PLANET BEAR

SHIFTER'S WORLD #1

REBECCA ROYCE

Planet Bear (Shifter's World #1)

Copyright @ 2018 by Rebecca Royce

First publication: 2018 by After Glows Publishing

Ebook ISBN: 978-1-947672-65-9

Cover art by Virginia Nelson

Content Editing: Heather Long

Copy Editing: Bookends Publishing

Formatting: Ripley Proserpina

Published by Rebecca Royce

www.rebeccaroyce.com

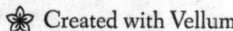 Created with Vellum

Dearest Reader

Thank you so much for picking up Planet Bear. If you have been following my career, you know this book was published with a publisher where it was the first in a line of fairytale retellings. Well, in the way of the world, I decided the best thing for me to do was to take back this story and republish it myself, making it the first book in trilogy about shifter worlds.

I hope you enjoy Planet Bear and be on the lookout for Planet Cat coming soon.

Thanks for reading
Rebecca Royce

CHAPTER 1

I STARED at the readings the SS *Goldie's* mainframe computer displayed and then checked them again. The information coming over the monitor couldn't be right. I shook my head but that didn't change the data the computer spit out. I sighed and leaned back in my seat.

This was my first mission working for *Union Delivery*, and I'd be damned if I screwed the pooch so badly they never gave me another one. Flight school graduation had been one week earlier. Union Delivery was my first real job and a simple one. Or so all my classmates claimed when they undertook their missions. Granted, I was first in my class, but the readout I'd received seemed downright ridiculous.

I turned in the chair and spoke to *The Goldie*. "Computer, send a message to Commandant Miranda from Jessica White." The fact that the delivery system still expected us to address ourselves and didn't automatically do it was one of the last antiquated problems with the ship-to-ship communications. "Let her know that I am questioning my orders. I think something is wrong."

"Affirmative." *Goldie* had a soothing voice that had been designed specifically to fit my psychological profile. Every ship in the fleet sounded a little bit different. If I were to get stuck in intergalactic space travel on someone else's vessel, it was entirely possible I'd be irritated and unhappy the whole time, based on the sound of the ship's voice alone. Or so the data suggested to the people in charge. I wished they'd spent as much time fixing the comms as they had designing happy computer voices.

I really didn't care about niceties, just convenience. I'd traveled space for as long as I could remember. Certainly longer than I should have been. The laws about how much time minors could spend off planet were meant to stop kids from having just the kind of upbringing I'd had. My Uncle Mac had believed in things like rules and regulations for other people, but not when it came to his own ship. Many a night, he'd gone to bed, leaving either Calvin or me in charge. Now, if the authorities had ever found out, he could have been in serious trouble, but the Whites were a family that never did anything halfway. We either managed to avoid trouble or die from an overdose of it.

The jury was still out on which one of those fates I would turn out to have.

I was, at least, trying to walk—or fly—the straight and narrow. I worked for the government. Not against it.

Goldie beeped, and I checked Commandant Miranda's reply.

I checked the orders twice when I saw them and threw them back to command. That's why you had to wait for so long. Command feels that with your special flying abilities, you don't need to be held back. It would be a waste of resources. You can do this. Be careful in shifter space. Other-

wise everything is the same as any other delivery. You can do this.

Should I be concerned that the commandant felt compelled to tell me I could do this more than once? I sighed. Again. Even Uncle Mac, before he had blown to smithereens in a space battle with a rival pirate, hadn't ventured to shifter space. Every good pilot knew that. The shifters didn't allow non-shifters onto their planets. Landing was a death sentence, and crash landing was no excuse. The biggest problem? The space that wound through the tri-fold shifter worlds were brutal, and the solar flares from the three rotating suns played havoc with onboard systems.

A pilot had to be an expert on all things space travel to hold their ship steady and straight.

All of this meant it was a really good idea to simply avoid the region altogether. The shifters—bear, wolf, and giant cats—had outlawed the use of their own spaceships for anything other than defense. But destroying anyone who dared penetrate their borders didn't seem to bother them.

So, of course the Union had gone and terraformed planets on both sides of their systems. Someone had to deliver goods and manage the trade.

It looked like one of those someones was going to be me.

The folks at the Union who determined our assignments—and I highly suspected it was one dude in a room somewhere—weren't wrong. I could get this ship back and forth across shifter space. I'd done it before. Of course, I'd never wanted to do it again. The dampening systems had gone haywire, and it had been the roughest ride of my life. But I'd done it.

I guess that mattered more to my bosses than my newbie status.

I sighed. They gave extra pay to the pilots who made

these runs. Maybe that would mean that I could actually afford to buy my brother out of jail this month instead of next. I gritted my teeth. Stupid jackass was why I was in this situation to begin with. We were going to live quietly, somewhere on a planet with no one around who could involve us in any nonsense that might end with us getting blown up. Then the stupid idiot had to go and get himself arrested.

And I got to fly through shifter space.

Asshat.

Pilots didn't know what they carried. It was our job to just get it where it belonged, and whatever I was carrying must need to be in the new colonies. I'd never found putting off anything made it any better. I had an uncomfortable thing to do. I might as well get it done and make it a memory. I could put this in the back of my brain where I shoved everything else I hated thinking about. I'd make this trip one of those 'yep not thinking about it' things too.

I programmed in the coordinates. For now, autopilot would do just fine. I bit my fingernail.

Shifter space on my first day employed by the respectable Union. No one would believe me, even if I was allowed to talk about this, which of course I wasn't. Breaking non-disclosure agreements could mean death. I wasn't getting executed or destroyed. Not if I could manage not to. I was going to find my little planet somewhere, and I was going to see to it I stayed in one piece. That was all I ever wanted.

It was a full twenty-four hours of nothing special happening before I got to the edge of shifter space. Earth space was always busy, but well patrolled. I didn't need to worry too much about space traffic. Other pilots kept to themselves and their designated lanes. It wasn't until I got a little farther out showboating happened. Pilots liked to stretch their legs, and even though I wasn't likely to do anything stupid, I'd been known to speed on occasion. I liked the way the ship moved, I liked how it responded to my commands. I liked the control, and okay, I liked the thrill of it.

But I had no need for any of that this time. I was going into shifter space.

I'd have plenty of things to hold my attention for about eight hours before I could let my guard down.

I held on to the controls and took the ship off autopilot. More fools died in this area of space trying to keep the ship on autopilot than any other mistake. I was many things, but foolish wasn't one of them. Not anymore.

The truth was, the shifter planets were gorgeous. Blue. Green. They had almost no pollution. Earth might look like them if we hadn't nearly destroyed it during the dark years. Ugh, I had no time for these thoughts. I needed to concentrate.

Goldie's controls were steady. One hand on the thruster, I kept it from increasing against the space winds. It was such a bizarre stream in this area of the universe, as though it either wanted to push me forward, jerk me right, left, or destroy me all together. I shook my head. There I went, personifying inanimate objects again.

I was a good pilot but the rest of my brain—yeah not so smart. The winds didn't want anything. They were a space phenomenon that no one could solve because they couldn't spend enough time to research them in the region. Thank you, shifters.

Sweat broke out on the back of my neck as though I somehow knew *Goldie* was about to start shaking seconds before she actually did. I sighed. I'd wanted this ship when no one else in my graduating class had. She was old. But then again, so was I. In my group of twenty graduates, I was the eldest of the bunch. The ripe old age of twenty-five put me four to five years senior to everyone else in the class.

Of course, they didn't have my life experience and were probably taking nice little runs from Earth to Mars without having to pass by a bunch of shifting to animal lunatics on either side of them.

Hours felt like minutes and somehow also like years. Sweat drenched my body. I gripped the controls. If I could will the ship to stay like this—shimmying but not breaking apart—I'd do it. My stomach clenched as nausea rolled through me. Space travel was usually boring.

A loud boom sounded, my first indication that I'd been shot. What in the hell? I was still in the passage that allowed us to move through this system. I hadn't strayed even a little bit over. Boom. Again. This time I was able to tell that the firing was coming from Wolf Planet.

"Fuck. Me." I screamed before I pressed the button to give Goldie instruction. "Goldie, tell the Union I've taken fire and. . ." I realized I didn't know how bad off I was. The controls were going haywire. I couldn't make out any of the readings. Looked like I was in a spin, but who could tell. I was being sucked into. . . "I'm going to crash land on Planet Bear."

Oh, that was bad. Technically, it wasn't called Planet Bear. It was something more sophisticated, but we called it after the shifters occupying it. And who gave a shit about that now? I was going down onto it, which meant that I was officially going to be a White that went kablooey. Bear defense would make sure that if the crash didn't kill me, they would.

Damn it. I wanted the quiet existence and the minding

my own business part of this life. I wasn't even notorious, hadn't earned what was coming for me. Maybe this was some kind of family karma. I bellowed out my fear. I wouldn't go afraid. That much I would promised myself. All the way to my end, I'd be brave. This was so damn unfair.

I held on to *Goldie* tightly. What else really was there to do?

———

I thought the alarms finally woke me. *Goldie's* proximity warnings must have gone off sometime upon entering the atmosphere, but I couldn't remember exactly. My head hurt. I clutched my forehead. Blood seeped through my fingers, dripping onto my broken console.

How had I gotten here, and why wasn't I dead? I undid the belt holding me in the chair and rose. *Goldie* was a mess. She wouldn't be salvageable. There were more problems than I cared to figure out right then, none the least of which was half the ship seemed to be missing. Several tree branches had taken down the top hatches, and an entire wall of the hull was gone, simply sheared away. Gold bars were strewn all over the control room, which at least let me know what had been in the cargo bay. No wonder the Union had been in a right old hurry. I sunk back down in the chair as dizziness assaulted me. I was clearly concussed, and there wasn't a damned thing I could do about it.

Damn it, I'd crash-landed on Planet Bear. How fucked was I?

Tears I'd refused to shed earlier—I thought, anyway, since there was a whole chunk of missing time in my head I didn't know for sure—rushed out. Well, this just plain sucked. Sucked. Sucked. Sucked.

How was I still here? The bear air security should have blown me out of the sky while I'd been descending. And yet. . .

Okay, I'd sent an SOS to the Union. They'd at least come to see what happened to me and do a preliminary scan for my remains and their gold. Maybe not in that order.

Despite the fact that the world tilted backward and forward, making me want to puke, I pulled myself into a standing position. I was alive. That was weird, but I wasn't going to complain. If the universe wasn't done fucking with me yet, then I'd just go for it, as per usual. Maybe I was on my way to becoming notorious. Maybe I'd be the first human woman to crash on Planet Bear and return to talk about it. I grabbed several gold bars, taking them one at a time, since they were heavy. They usually had tracking on them. When the Union found their gold, they could also locate me.

Plan decided, I grabbed the bag hanging from the back of my chair and shoved the gold in. The whole kitchen area of the ship was gone. I'd have to find food and water.

What did I know about the bear shifters who lived here? Nothing. Nothing at all. All my uncle ever said was stay the heck away from shifter space. I'd gotten away with it once. Twice, not so likely.

They were dangerous enough the Union respected their borders, which was all the information I needed. I had to figure out how to hide until help came—however long that took. Anything else would mean death for sure. Since I'd already somehow managed to cheat my own demise once today, maybe the universe was on my side.

Or maybe I was delusional. Dying in a crash would

have been painless—hadn't I been unconscious when I hit? Maybe the universe said 'psych!' With bear shifters somewhere out there, I couldn't afford to get cocky.

I exited the ship, leaving it as fast as I could manage on foot. Smoke bellowed upward. Whatever set of circumstances had allowed me to survive, I wasn't going to stick around the wreckage and let the creatures find me. I sucked in a deep breath as *fresh* air and dizziness assailed me again. Concussion, or something in the air itself? A thought dawned on me. Not every planet was kind to human lungs. Was this one? Did the shifters simply breathe differently? Was this all just psychosomatic?

I forced myself to calm. I was breathing. If I couldn't, I'd be dead already. Who knew how long I'd been out cold in that chair? The ship had gaping holes. I'd been breathing the air a long time. I was fine. I had to be smart. I could survive. I had twenty-five years of experience to draw on.

I'd kept my brother and myself alive for a year in the woods before our uncle found us after my parents had been blown up in a bizarre barn fire that had sent the whole structure into the atmosphere of the planet they'd been trying to raise us on, landing them and the barn who knew where. They'd been dead. Or at least it had seemed that way since they'd never come back. Our house on that planet —that had turned out to be not at all safe—had gone up in that blaze too. We'd had to eat berries and hunt animals to survive. Sometimes, we'd been so hungry I hadn't known how we would make it. But I'd done it. I'd kept us alive.

I could do the same here. I'd just have to be tough and smart, again. . .

Blood continued to ooze from the head wound. Swiping the stinging flow away from my eyes didn't do much, but passing out again would be really, *really* bad. Nearby woods drew my attention, and I ran hard and fast for them. My injury and blood loss made this a lot harder than it should have been, but I gritted my teeth and kept going, losing track of time. I moved until I had to stop for a breather. I rested, and then I ran some more. I ate things that I hoped weren't poisonous plants. I never ran into another living soul anywhere. If I'd been focused on anything before I fled the ship, I'd have grabbed a protein bar. Clearly, my concussion had knocked the sense out of me too. Gold bars, yes. Food, no.

Maybe everything we knew about Planet Bear was wrong. Maybe it was actually completely devoid of people. Maybe...

My mind had really started to play havoc on me, and I needed to settle it down. I had to find some real food, some protein that I could put in my stomach. But that was going to be easier thought than done. My hunting skills without a weapon were zilch. My father's shotgun had made it through the blast that took him out, falling from the sky, but the bullets hadn't come down with it. I'd been able to feed us better then than I could take care of myself now.

I stumbled into a clearing and then darted backward. I needed to be calculating, to make sure there were no bears waiting to eat me. I inched toward it with hunger and desperation making me bolder with each step. I stopped abruptly on the edge of the forest, almost unable to believe my eyes. There was a house. An actual house. Tears flooded my eyes, and I pushed them away.

Seeing a house wasn't necessarily a good thing. That meant there were bear shifters around. I clung to a tree on the edge of the woods. If they found me, I was dead.

I waited a while, watching the house. It was the middle of the day. Did bear shifters work? The house was alone, the only one I could see in any distance. Maybe it was some kind of country home that no one used. Maybe my concussion wasn't better. Maybe it was empty. Maybe there was food around. Maybe I was really crazy enough to go find out.

I ducked, although I wasn't exactly sure why. I was the only moving object around, and at five foot ten, I wasn't exactly small. Someone could see me if they just glanced out the window. A dusting of rain hit me, and I was suddenly extremely glad the last however many days, weeks, years that I'd been here had been good weather, pleasant outside and not too cold at night.

That might all be changing.

I ran as quickly as I could manage to the edge of the house, breathing hard. Tiredness weighed on my shoulders, but hunger came first. I pressed my head against the window. The lights were on, but no people. I ran to the next window and did the same. Perhaps calling the structure a house was pushing the definition. This place was a mansion. An estate. It took me half an hour of cautiously ducking around windows and trying not to be seen to circle it, and the entire time, I saw no one inside. The fact that it didn't look abandoned—the lights were on and there were occasional pieces of clothing thrown over the backs of chairs —was both concerning and great news. The first, because they could come back at any time, and the second, because that meant there might be food.

I made my decision and refused to overthink it. I was getting in there. I tried the door, fully expecting it to be locked. They had a lot of stuff to be protected from invaders like me. All of it looking very human. The whys of that I would figure out at a later time, if ever. Maybe I'd never think about this period of my life ever again. Or it could feel like a nightmare I'd soon get over.

The door handle turned. The door creaked open. My hands shook, and I shoved them in my pockets. A war raged in my head, and I didn't know what to do about it. I needed to go in. I had to find something to eat and maybe also steal something to protect me from the elements while I waited.

But I hadn't been invited. We'd been poor on our colony planet, but my mother had taught me manners and my uncle had his own brand of morality he'd pounded into us. I'd never been in a huge house like this one. I almost felt like I should take off my shoes and leave them at the door.

I sighed. The occupants of this house could return any time. I couldn't afford to dally. No siree Bob. I rushed forward like my life depended on it and made my way to the kitchen. I'd seen it from outside. I knew where it was. I tracked dirt onto the floor, which made me wince. Someone was going to have to clean up after me.

The bear shifters had what looked like a giant freezer with a small fridge beneath it. Very different than the traditional way humans did it. Perhaps they needed food to stay better for longer periods of time? Oh hell, what did it matter? I flung open the fridge part and grabbed the first thing I saw. It seemed like some kind of porridge.

I pushed it into my mouth, using my hands like some kind of savage. We had manners, if nothing else, in my family, but all of that had gone out the window with my starvation. This was probably not the protein I needed. Still, it tasted like heaven all wrapped up in one delicious bowl. There was a small trace of honey to it.

I rushed over to the sink and placed the bowl down. Okay, next I would look for. . .

"Stop." A low, masculine voice sounded in the room. I whirled around. The tallest man I'd ever seen—he must be an entire foot bigger than me—stared down at me. He was shirtless, wearing only shorts, and his hair was wet like he'd just gotten out of the shower. I hadn't heard anyone coming. Then again, I'd been a little busy feeding myself like a maniac.

"I'm sorry." That was the only thing I could think to say to the brown haired, brown eyed, thick eyebrowed giant. He had muscles for his muscles. Yes, he probably ate human women for a snack, and he wouldn't even have to shift to do it.

His pupils changed. That was the only way I could describe what happened for the few seconds that his gaze changed from the dark brown look of a man confused about what was happening in his kitchen to the look of a bear that found some woman in his cave. Or wherever it was that bears slept.

The giant cocked his head to the side for a second and took a deep breath. The gaze changed right back.

I held up my hands. "Please don't kill me. I'll go back to the woods. No one will know I was ever here. My people will come for the gold. They'll take me with them. End of story."

He took a second to answer me. "You're who they're looking for. The pilot who crashed here. A small woman. They're not reporting that part. Interesting. Amazing what humans let their women do."

I almost launched into my equal rights speech, and then I thought better of it. I'd call him a misogynist in my own head and leave it at that. Time and place, Jessica. Time and place. "I'm the one. I didn't mean to come here. Planet Wolf shot at me for no reason. I was in the registered lane. I thought I would die in the crash or you guys would kill me. I didn't mean to be here."

He still hadn't moved. "You smell. . ." He didn't finish that thought, instead running a hand through his hair. "This is going to be complicated."

"You're telling me. I'm sorry. Please let me go. I'm sorry I tracked dirt. I'm sorry I ate your food."

He pointed to my head. "You're hurt. Badly."

"Maybe. I don't know." I backed up. Maybe I could run for it. How fast were bears?

The owner of the house shook his head. "My attempts to calm you are not working. So, I'll just say it. Be rid of your fear, human woman. You are not in danger from me, and you will not be in danger from my brothers, although they've yet to return and don't know about you. I can guarantee it. You will not go into the woods. You're hungry." He pointed to the table. "Sit in a chair. I'll feed you."

I didn't move. "Are you just waiting until authorities arrive to take me away or shoot me on sight?"

"I'm the authority, mate. And no one is taking you anywhere."

What had he just called me? My knees gave out. I'd never fainted in my entire life, but there was a first time for everything.

CHAPTER 2

"THERE NOW, SMALL ONE. WAKE UP." A voice called to me, as someone raised my head and touched my forehead with something warm. "You are not so injured that you need to be taken to an infirmary. You simply need to open your eyes. We'll get you feeling much better."

I forced my lids open. I didn't know the voice that spoke, but I immediately recognized one of the three faces staring down at me. The giant from the kitchen and two more, whose high cheekbones had to signify they were the brothers he'd mentioned. Unless all bear shifters looked like that. Maybe they did. Brown hair. Brown eyes. High cheekbones. The one closest to me had a slightly more rounded face, and the third man, who stood next to the one I'd sort of met, had a cleft in his chin.

The closest of them, presumably the one who had been speaking to me, put a straw to my mouth, and I sipped. Water rushed down my throat quickly, and I nearly choked, which had him pulling the drink away from me.

"Slowly. You're dehydrated, and you fainted. Exhaustion, maybe. I don't like your head injury. Your physiology is the same as ours in this state. You're just fragile. Don't fret. We'll see to it that you are okay from here on in."

The third one spoke. "You're sure, Cole? I won't risk her. I mean, I don't understand how this is happening, but it is, so I won't allow anything to happen to her. She's so small. So likely to break."

"She is fragile, for sure. But maybe tougher than she looks at the same time," the one who had been called Cole answered. "She did survive out there somehow on her own, and we're nowhere near the wreckage." He rose from the bed. "You need food and maybe something to make your head stop hurting since you can't shift."

Shift. The word made me want to pull the covers up over my head and hide. That wouldn't do me any good, but it was everything I could do in the world not to simply give in and hide under the blankets. The first guy had told me I was safe and then used the word mate. I didn't know what customs and rules were on this planet or with their species, but there were all kinds of ways to hurt someone.

I swallowed. My throat was still dry, but I forced myself to speak. "What are you going to do with me? Or to me?"

The three of them stared at each other for a long second before they all turned to look at me. First guy spoke. "I've told her that she would be safe here. That I was in charge of what would happen. She didn't hit her head when she fell, but perhaps the crash? That bump and the cut? Do you suppose she has brain damage?"

"I don't have brain damage." I sat up straight in the bed, which was when it occurred to me that I was in bed. I guessed that answered my cave question. They slept in beds. Or at least they had one. I had to keep track of what I'd been saying. "It's a reasonable question. I am here illegally, but not purposefully. I don't wish to cause any harm. I'm sorry I stole your porridge. I. . ."

I took a deep breath. "You said I was safe, but then you used that word—mate—and I am not going to do that just because I took the porridge. I have gold in my bag. I'll pay you."

The third one held up his hand. He spoke to his brother. "We're having a meaning of the word problem. That means something different to them, and she can't understand scent as we do."

First guy made a noise in his throat that sounded like a growl. "Okay. We'll start over. I did bumble it. I was in the shower. The aroma hit me. It was all I could do to get down the stairs and not destroy things to do so. You had the same reaction. You might have made mistakes too if she had been conscious when you got here."

Cole sighed. "Hold on, you two. Please. You'll have to excuse my brothers. Oldest and youngest. They bicker while I make peace. We are the Durojo family. You are in our house. You met Finn first. He was here when you arrived." First guy nodded to me. "He is the oldest of our family and the leader of this planet. I'm Cole. I have some medical skills. That is why I examined you. And my youngest brother, Rylan. He's actually been looking for you for several days. You managed to elude him. You'll have to tell him sometime how you did that. And he'll have to tell us why he kept the fact that he scented what you would be to us to himself."

"Hasn't exactly been the time." Rylan growled, his voice lowering. "It is illegal. I wasn't going to discuss it with strangers. I was waiting until the three of us could be alone."

I got up on my knees. I understood about half of what

they were talking about, but I wasn't worried about it. The fundamentals of things had not changed. I had to get out of here before whatever they smelled caused them to hurt me.

"I'm sorry I'm here. I'm sorry I came in here uninvited. I can go. You never have to see me again."

Finn scrunched up his face. "We're not angry. Relieved, in some ways. And confused. But not upset." He patted the top of my leg. "I was going to feed you. I scent hunger from you, and if we are to proceed, in whatever way we can possibly do that, then I need to make sure you are cared for first."

Rylan laughed. "You were going to cook? You don't cook."

"Maybe I was going to warm something. I would have gotten her fed."

I shook my head. "I think we're having a little bit of a translation problem." They all turned to stare at me when I said that. Okay, that was good. They could take me seriously. I had a chip in my ear that let me hear in my own language. Although these shifters hated people from other planets, presumably they must have them, too, since they could hear me just fine. Otherwise, planet-to-planet, and sometimes within one planet itself, people would struggle to make themselves understood.

Still, things went askew. This had to be one of those times. I pointed to my ear. "I'm hearing things that don't make sense, and that is fine. That happens. My name is Jessica White. I work for the Union as a courier. I bring things through space. Well, this was my first mission." Rylan opened and closed his mouth. I didn't know what he was going to say or why he decided not to speak. Or maybe that was some kind of tic thing he did. It didn't matter right then.

I had their attention, so I continued. "I was flying

through the assigned corridor of space, and the wolves shot some kind of planet to space missile and knocked me off the corridor and sent me crashing onto your planet. I don't really remember anything from after the strike until I woke. I was pretty sure I was going to die. My family tends to be blown up in lots of different ways, but the end result is the same. We just do."

Cole rubbed his chin and rocked back on his feet, but he didn't interrupt. I really appreciated them not talking over me. Whatever the glitch was in our language chips, we could overcome it if we just all listened very carefully.

"I know that you guys, as a rule, don't allow non shifters here. That is fine. I don't want to be here. My people will come get me. I can either wait until they do somewhere else, or maybe you could contact them." I might have been expendable, and I really hoped I wasn't, but the gold would get them here fast. "You can all go back to your lives."

Cole shook his head. "I am going to go do the cooking. You can explain this, Rylan. Finn needs to call off the searchers."

I rubbed my eyes. Why weren't they focusing on the fundamentals here?

Rylan sat down on the bed next to me, patting my leg under the blanket. "Are you in pain? Cole wanted to get you a pain block. I can do that."

"I am in pain, but I'm less concerned about that than about the things I said not being answered. I am grateful you are trying to help me. Concerned, but grateful." There. I'd been magnanimous, hadn't I? I knew big words sometimes. I could read and did when I had any time.

"Listen, this must be confusing. It is for us too." Rylan sighed. "You see, we were raised to believe humans smelled bad. That upon encountering a human, we would instantly want to kill it."

It. I tried not to wince, but failed. His use of that term was exactly what I was afraid of. I was a cockroach to them. Every planet had them. The little bastards probably had their own interstellar travel arrangements.

He made a growling noise in the back of his throat and then abruptly stopped. "I didn't mean to say what I said the way I said it. I'm not. . .good at this. Finn should be explaining. Okay, listen, we *don't* hate the way you smell. If anything, we're sort of addicted to it. You smell like our mate. I don't know what you know about us since we know little about you, but we mate as clans. Brothers usually mate the same woman. There are always more males than females. Our kind evolved that way. Helps us protect you better too. You're ours."

My mouth fell open. "That's not possible. I'm not a bear shifter." Now at least I understood that word Finn had used. "Bear shifters must mate other bear shifters."

"Yes. Usually. But we don't often find ourselves with others outside of our population. You'll adjust to the idea. You'll like us. We are the strongest clan on the planet. Finn is in charge. It's an honor to be our mate."

I'd had enough. I couldn't be reasonable. My head pounded. Fear made me stupid. I'd used up all my reserves to keep my freak out from coming.

"No." Okay, I shouted. I did. I'll admit it. "No. No. No." I repeated myself over and over. I wasn't going to stay here. I wasn't going to adjust. This just wasn't happening. I shoved at the big brick wall that was Rylan. He didn't budge with my attempted assault. Instead, his eyes changed, like Finn's had earlier.

One second, his dark brown depths were human, and

the next, they weren't. Finn's had immediately changed back, but Rylan's weren't.

"You will hurt yourself." His voice was low, much deeper than earlier. He rose to his feet. "I won't let you do that."

Finally, I grabbed the blanket, and I threw it over my head. I'd had a temper tantrum, and now I was hiding like a child under the blankets. Maybe they'd decide I wasn't worth all this hassle and kick me out. That would work just fine by me.

The bed was too big. I wasn't used to having so much space, and when I was really lost in the universe, I liked to feel squished. There was too much room around me for things to happen.

The bed dipped. Rylan must have sat back down. "You're frightened."

Did he expect me to answer? I had nothing to say about that. Zilch. Nada. Yes, I was terrified. "Imagine if you were unexpectedly on Earth or one of the human colonies somewhere and someone said you could never leave. That you belonged to them. What would you do? You wouldn't be scared?"

He tugged on the blanket, but only so much as to get my attention, not to pull it off me. "Well, to start, I would probably have done less well than you did avoiding capture. How did you do that?"

I pushed the blanket aside. His eyes were still bear-like. Huge and brown, unhuman, not matching his very male and terran looking figure. "I don't know. I don't know how I didn't die in the crash. I don't know how I avoided being caught. All of it was accidental. I'm a good pilot. I've survived in the woods before, but that's about it. I don't know."

"We'll figure it out another time. Let's just focus on the basics right now."

I let him take my hand and lead me from the room. They were all very preoccupied with getting me fed, and I wasn't going to object. Not if I had to run away, which I did, in order to not have to belong to them. What did that mean? What would their expectations of me be? Cleaning? Cooking? Sex? I had plans, and damn it, they didn't include this level of crazy.

I sat down in a chair that was way too big for me, and a second later, Cole stood in front of me, placing a plate down. I stared at it for a second. "This looks a lot like a fish we have on Earth called salmon."

"I imagine you have a lot of the same foods we do." Cole sat down next to me. "Because we gave them to you when we deposited your ancestors on the terraformed planet many, many millenniums ago."

I jolted at his words. "What?"

"Or so the legends go. My limited understanding of the non-shifting species is you think the same of us. What is it? We evolved here differently because of the moon?" He pointed at the salmon-like fish. "You'll tell me how you like it or if you don't?"

I took a bite. It was a warm, subtle experience, more like meat than fish. Yes, it was very close to our Earth salmon, yet it also had more of an aftertaste to it. I took another bite and then nodded. Belonging to them apparently meant being fed well. "Thank you."

"You like it?" He pressed.

I nodded. "I do. Thank you."

"You're welcome." He grinned. "I very rarely cook it. I can't hear what you call it, by the way. I just hear what we call it when you speak. The chip." He pointed to his ear. "We have gotten into a habit of eating in our bear form. Grabbing the fish and eating it right there. Bad manners, my mother would have said. We eat in our human skin, my mother used to say. But the three of us have been without female companionship since our mother passed, and I'm afraid we have forgotten how to be. Like, for example, how Rylan needs to sit his ass down."

Cole's speech made Rylan drop down into chair next to me. "Sorry."

"Don't mind him. He's young." Cole grinned at me. "He's still learning."

"I'm almost one hundred years old, asshole."

Cole ignored him. "Ninety-eight. Those last two years make all the difference. It's why he can't shift his eyes back. The bear wants out, and he's battling to keep it in."

Rylan gripped the edge of the table. "I have it well in hand."

"If you say so."

My appetite fled, and I set down my fork. I'd never been able to eat through fear, unless it was chocolate. I could eat chocolate in any circumstance. Not that I'd had any since the Union banned it. No booze. No chocolate. No garlic. Nothing fried. All the things I liked in life.

Cole's face fell. "You're afraid."

"She stopped being that way for maybe two seconds, and then you scared her again."

I hated being talked about like I wasn't in the room. "When you're a bear, will you tear me to pieces? Will it hurt?" Why did I add that? Stupidest question ever. Of course it would hurt. "Are you fattening me up so that I taste better?"

No one spoke for a second. Oh wow, I'd really stepped

in it. Why couldn't I keep quiet until I had a chance to escape? Because I was dumb, dumb, dumb. That was why.

"Not one of us would ever hurt you in either form. You belong to us." If it was possible, Rylan's voice lowered further.

I pushed back from the table. "What does that mean? What will you expect me to do?" I must not have gotten over my hysterics from earlier because it reared back at me like it had just been waiting to smack me into this zone once again. "Clean? Cook? Things in the bedroom? You have to explain it."

"It's different with humans." Finn leaned against the door to the kitchen. "She can't smell us. They use the word differently, I think. It's been a long time since I gave a human a thought other than to have them executed for being here when they shouldn't."

I backed up two more steps. They'd catch me if I ran. That didn't mean I wasn't going to try. Why couldn't I have found a different house where the bears didn't want to keep me?

Rylan rose slowly. "She is so afraid. It burns my senses."

"Tell the bear to go away. The scent eases a little bit in human form." Finn walked toward me slowly. "I don't want you afraid, little human, so I will tell you all the things that might frighten you all at once. Then we will soothe you."

Soothe me? He had to be kidding. "I don't think there's anything you can say that is going to make any of this better."

"Maybe not." Finn stalked forward. "But let's get it all on the table. They aren't hunting for you anywhere because I made a general announcement that you'd been found. It will be a little while until one group starts to wonder why they don't have you and why another group does. By then, we'll have to figure out how we're going to handle this. We can't go into hiding. You're our mate. You belong to us."

There were those words again. "What does that *mean*? I'm sure there must be a better candidate for a mate."

Finn looked at Cole and then back at me. "The second I scented you, your aroma hitting me upstairs when you were down here, my bear knew you were ours. I knew my brothers would feel it too. That's how it works. We will suit. So, no, there aren't better candidates. Trust me. Mothers have been throwing their daughters in the path of our clan since Rylan hit adulthood, hoping her scent would awaken the mating. You did."

If this wasn't happening to me, I might find it interesting. "I don't want it."

Rylan made a noise, and Finn winced. I turned to see what was happening. Cole rose, a groan sounding from him. A second later, with no warning, Rylan's body started to change.

"He can't always control it yet. The ability to stave off the bear when the bear wants out comes in the second hundred years. Mine was actually on my birthday. About one hundred years ago."

Two hundred years. Finn was two hundred years old? Or more? I retreated another step. Rylan's body reshaped, fur pushing out where there hadn't been, and with a snap, suddenly the largest grizzly bear I'd ever seen was in the room with us. Not that I had ever seen one outside of a zoo or in pictures. In any case, I knew that was a grizzly bear.

The high ceilings in this place made sense. They had to fit in it when they were a bear.

He dropped to four feet, walking toward me, and I officially slammed into the wall in my haste, pressing myself against it. My heart beat so loudly I could hear it in my ears.

This was it. He was a bear now, and he was simply going to rush at me, swat me down, and eat me while I was still alive. That was what bears did. My uncle must have told me that. Or maybe not. It didn't matter. At some point in my life, I had picked up that information.

Only, he stopped moving when he was right next to Finn. Cole walked up on his other side. "She can't smell you, Rylan. She doesn't know that you mean her no harm. There's nothing you could do to him that would cause him to hurt you. You're the only person in the universe that is true for. He's deadly." He stared at me for a second, consternation drawing his brows together. "That was supposed to make you feel better."

I shook my head. "Nope."

Rylan loped forward, stopping right in front of me. My body started to shake. I was way too close to a predator. If there was one thing I knew from simply surviving all these years, it was that some things out there killed you because that was what they did. Rylan the bear lowered his head, and I fully expected him to bite down. There was nothing I could do. This whole thing had been a game. And. . .he nuzzled against my shoulder.

I swallowed. Okay. That hadn't been what I was expecting. He raised his head and then did it again. It was nice, but I didn't trust it. Not yet. What did he want? "Can he understand me like this?"

"Sort of. Senses of what you're saying," Cole answered. "When Finn told him that you couldn't scent him, he sort of got that. He knows that we're talking now. Probably about him. Or at least, I would know that."

I sighed. "Please back up. I don't like this." I was lying. I did sort of like the heat of him, the way his nose felt when he nuzzled against me. I liked that he was being gentle. But

I didn't want him this close. Not when I had to find my feet, figure things out. I couldn't have a bear pressed up against me like this was normal. It wasn't. They had to understand I wasn't their mate.

I took a deep breath. He hadn't moved. Finn said I was safe. I was going to try to believe him. "Back up, please." I swatted him right on the nose.

Rylan made a grumbling noise and backed up before heading toward the back of the house. Cole ran ahead and opened the door, which the bear used to exit. I let out a breath I'd held.

Finn's eyebrows were raised. "Good job. He understood that. So would I. Nothing says go away more than your mate swatting you on the nose."

"I can't be your mate. Work with me here. Shouldn't this role be given to say a female bear shifter who could give you cubs? Isn't that how it should work in nature? You guys don't like strangers on your planet. You shouldn't be mating one."

Finn nodded. "Something is different, that is for sure. I've never been around a human before. All communication has been done over screens. You're supposed to smell awful. You don't. I think our parts are probably made to work just fine." He winked at me. "And if we can't have cubs—although I would probably say babies, maybe we're lost in translation—then that's just fine too. I don't care. You're ours."

I walked toward him. "You can't possibly meet a stranger and just suddenly think you're going to keep her and make her yours forever. I might be the worst person in the universe for all you know. I have terrible luck, for one thing. Life tends to send me explosions. You don't want to be anywhere near me."

"Whatever it is"—Cole walked toward Finn. They stood shoulder-to-shoulder—"you're ours. Even if we have to prove it to you."

I put my shaking hands in my pockets. I needed a shower. I had to think. I had to breathe. I couldn't do either of those things with them standing so close. Even Rylan, who was outside, was too close. I bent over, putting my hands on my knees. "Please."

That was all I could manage to say. Finn walked over, placing his hand on my back. The bear was back in his eyes. Cole squatted down in front of me. Like his brother, he wasn't using his human eyes. "Please what, mate?"

"I have to go." Why didn't they understand? "I don't belong here. You'll find a different mate."

They would. Cole touched the side of my face. "Jessica, you're safe. For now, hold on to that. Let's figure things out in the morning. Or the next morning. Or the one after that. Start with safe. Tomorrow tends to take care of itself."

He was wrong. The only tomorrows that took care of themselves were the ones I made sure were set up in advance. Otherwise, life was a giant mess all the time. It was clear they weren't to be reasoned with on this matter. I'd simply have to bide my time.

"Okay."

CHAPTER 3

WHEN I WAS fourteen years old, the authorities in the Mars colony put my brother Calvin and me in an orphanage. It had been more like a labor camp. Use the parentless to do labor no one else would do. I pushed away the memory. They'd arrested my uncle on some trumped up charge of pirating—the new mayor of the place didn't like his cut of the spoils—and kept us there until things were sorted out. After he'd been freed, my uncle picked us up and we'd gone on like nothing had happened at all.

Only, there were things that happened there, things that took place when adults weren't paying close enough attention, that had really shaped Calvin and me. My brother decided he needed to be the toughest guy in the room at all times, and I wanted nothing more than somewhere quiet where I could be left alone. After Cal went to jail and I had to take the piloting job with the Union to buy him out of his situation, I'd sworn I was almost to the place I wanted to be.

Little did I know I had to make this bear detour first.

One thing I'd learned in the orphanage was how to convince people I was asleep when I wasn't. I lay still in the bed and waited. The bears could hear better than me. I didn't even want to imagine how much more they could make out with their ears than mine, but that didn't mean I couldn't be sneaky if I was careful.

I'd gotten into the house when Finn had been in the shower. After I'd eaten Cole's delicious salmon, I'd taken a shower and gotten in the way too big bed that seemed to have been given to me. Or maybe I'd just assumed it was mine. In any case, I was using it for now. I kept the door to the room cracked, and every time I heard either Cole or Finn speak, I listened carefully. Rylan, it seemed, was still out in the North woods. Cole headed out to go search for him and bring him back. Finn needed to speak to the elders, whoever they were, about humans and why they'd been told we smelled badly.

I waited until I heard him leave. He crossed the downstairs, and not quietly, before he closed a door to communicate with whomever he needed to speak. My hair was still wet, but it was warm outside. I wouldn't freeze. I carefully made my way down the stairs. If Rylan and Cole were north, I'd head south.

It would be that easy. I stood at the threshold of the door that would lead me from the house, and I didn't move. What was the matter with me? I should just go. I put my hand on the wood. Truth was, I was tired. Bone weary. I was too young to be so tired. I just felt stretched thin.

I stepped back. Not tonight. I'd go to sleep and find another time to run when I had more energy.

"I'm glad you changed your mind." Rylan, in his human form, stood on the other side of the room. Cole came through the other door behind him. "It's not safe out there at night. I mean, I know you made it on your own, but I don't know how long you could have done that. There are bears—clanless bears that live in the woods. They wouldn't hesitate to harm you. I wouldn't let them. We'd kill anyone who came near you."

I cleared my throat. "In this scenario, I've run away."

"Couldn't happen. You're deep in our blood now. You evaded capture, a feat well done, and I suspect it's because we have all just come out of a torpor period. It makes us all a little bit off. That's why you didn't get shot down. That's why you lasted in the woods. But we're getting back to our normal rhythms. And we'd never lose your scent now. I'd rather not chase you tonight. I'd rather you just went to bed." He put out his hand. "Come on. I'll walk you back up."

Cole stepped past him. "You're really beautiful. This whole thing has been so bizarre I don't think we told you. You're beautiful. All that blond hair and those blue eyes. I wouldn't care what you looked like, but I love how you look. If that makes sense."

My cheeks heated. "I'm. . .I'm not beautiful."

Literally no one in my life had ever said that to me. My nose was too big. My eyes were slightly too far apart. It had never mattered. I'd never had boyfriends. How and when would I? And my one sexual experience had taught me I really didn't care for the intimacy anyway. What was the big deal?

I walked around Cole, who took my hand to stop me. "Sure, you are."

"What difference does it make?" I snapped at him. I did that a lot. Maybe they'd get rid of me for it. I was too volatile to be their mate.

He shook his head. "None."

Okay, he'd answered like I'd asked a reasonable question. What was I supposed to do with that? Rylan nudged me when he walked by. "Come on. Back to bed. It's been a long day. You're safe here." They kept reiterating that to me like it was going to make some kind of difference. "You can sleep. Nothing will happen to you."

I pointed out the window. "You just told me there are dangerous, non-clanned—whatever that means—bears in the wood. I think that negates the safety."

Still, I let him lead me upstairs like I couldn't find my own way.

Rylan answered my accusation. "They wouldn't dare come in here. If I didn't kill them, or Cole didn't kill them, Finn would make them wish they'd never been born. We can leave our doors unlocked because most of the time, except when beautiful blondes named Jessica stumble their way into our lives, no one would dare come in here uninvited."

Cole walked the other way down the long hall. "And we almost never invite anyone. We're bears. We like our own company."

"Well, you wouldn't know that considering you now seem to think I belong to you."

Cole's smile was huge. "You now constitute part of being us. Don't worry, you'll get used to the idea. My bear is sure of it."

I went back into my bedroom. This time, because I was at least spending the night, I took off my shoes. I grabbed a bar of the gold from my backpack and put it under my pillow. If any of them came at me, I could at least get a good whack in with the gold. It would hurt, even if I lost.

The bed was warm, and I'd rolled around in it, looking for a comfortable spot, when a knock sounded on the door. "Come in."

Cole poked his head in. "Sorry, you need the pain medicine." He held out a shot in his hand. "We don't have a lot of this. If a bear can't shift we give them this until they can. It lets them relax. I think this should be a low enough dose for you. I don't think there's any reason you shouldn't have it."

Bear pain killers? "I don't know."

"When we look like humans, our physiology is very close. I'd never give you anything unsafe. Hold out your arm."

I'd always hated injections, but I did as he asked. I really did need relief from my constant headache. It pinched but worked fast. My head was first a dull ache, and then I couldn't feel any pain at all. My neck felt weak. I leaned back on the pillow. "Thanks."

He gave me a small smile. "That is my pleasure. We'll all take care of you. Always."

I closed my eyes. I didn't have any fight left. I'd just float for a while. That sounded perfect.

I dreamed. Usually, I didn't recognize dreams as dreams when I was having them, but this one was clear. Was it something to do with the painkiller? I didn't know. I ran through the woods. Dangerous bears were everywhere. They chased me, swatting me with their claws. I ran straight into my uncle. He held me still.

"You're such a fuck up, girl. You're supposed to take care of Calvin. He's going to die in that jail because of you."

I cried out. "I'm going to get to him."

"You're not. You're never getting away from the bears. They're going to slaughter you right now."

I screamed, sitting up straight, the yell still in my throat. I was drenched in sweat. This had to be the painkiller. I never made a noise in my sleep. I'd learned in the orphanage the importance of silence. The door swung open, and Rylan was there.

He was quickly by the side of my bed. "Nightmare?"

I nodded. "Sorry. I don't remember when I last had one. I'm just screwed up."

He scooted in next to me. "I can't remember when I had one either." I moved over in the very large bed and let Rylan lie down on the side I'd moved from. "You're shaking." He put a hand on the top of my head. "You're okay. Must have been a bad one."

"It was a lot of things. My uncle yelling at me. My brother is in jail. I have to get him out. I have to pay for that." I choked on my words. Why was I telling him? I never talked about this. Not that I had all that many close friends. But even with the few I spoke to about my life, I didn't speak of my brother's situation. "And then there were all these bears that were going to kill me."

His voice was low in the darkness, his hand on my head. "That last part is my fault. I shouldn't have told you about the clanless."

"I have to know what's out there. It's not your fault. I have to protect myself."

Rylan scooted slightly closer to me. "No, you don't. That's our job. Finn, Cole, and I will always see to it that you are never harmed."

"For the next seventy-five years, if I'm lucky. Probably less. My family tends to get killed in particularly explosive ways. But let's say I live to be old. For the next seventy-five years you'll keep me safe?"

He sucked in his breath. "Is that all you could live? Seventy-five years?"

"Yes. That would make me one hundred years old. That's about all I could ask for. Truth is, that would be lucky. If I make it to my sixties, I made it a good long time."

He shook his head. "No, that's not acceptable. That's not enough time."

"How old will you become?" I knew he was almost one hundred and his brothers were older.

"Three hundred fifty, maybe four hundred. No, you can't only have thirty-five more years. Now I'm going to have nightmares." He drew me to him. "We have to really hurry up the you getting over your fear. Every day has to count."

I groaned. "I can't stay. I've just told you about my brother. Maybe I'm the wrong mate. Maybe it's a human thing. Maybe hundreds and hundreds of years ago, your ancestors realized that humans gave off a false mating signal. So, they decided to get rid of humans from the planet. Maybe every bear I encounter will think I'm their mate. You'd do best to send me off and find your true mate."

He was quiet. A pang pressed against my heart. I didn't want to be forced to stay because they wanted me to be their mate. But I didn't want their love of how I smelled to be because all humans tasted like chocolate cake to their nostrils.

"If any bear outside of this clan tried to take you, they would die. I wouldn't even wait for them to be dead to tear at them. I don't remember everything when I shift. But I would know that. We won't let anyone take you from us." He was quiet. "After you fell asleep, Cole reminded Finn and me that you're not a shifter. You're human. Maybe that's too savage. But it's true."

It should have been too much. But there in the dark, all I did was tug on his shirt and let him hold me tightly. I'd wonder why tomorrow.

Not tonight.

The door flung open, and a bear walked in. I gasped. I'd

only seen Rylan shifted, and he was next to me. Which one was this? "Is it one from the woods?"

"No, they'd never come here. They'd be dead by now. That's Finn. I'm shocked he's shifted. I can't remember the last time he was."

He jumped up on the other side of the bed, and I gasped, throwing myself into Rylan's arms. The bear grunted.

"He has claws out."

Rylan kissed my hair. "We don't retract them. Ever. It's okay. He's. . .tired. I can smell it. He's just here to sleep."

The bear lay down on his side, and the bed dipped. No wonder they had to be so big. He grunted again and then hit me with his nose, nuzzling like Rylan had done. He closed his eyes.

Rylan laughed, a low sound. "A million people would kill to see my brother like this. He's never this relaxed."

"I'm going to sleep in a bed with a bear."

Rylan's smile was fast. This close, I could see it through the low light of the door. "Two. You're going to sleep with two. And you'll never be better protected in your life."

If he said so. Still, the bed was warm, and with two of them there, it didn't feel quite so big. Eventually, I must have fallen asleep.

I didn't have any more dreams.

I woke up, light filling the room, and the sounds of two snoring males filling the quiet. One was a bear. The other wore a human form. And both of them snored, loudly.

I lay there listening. Yesterday hadn't been a dream. Rylan's head was near mine in the bed, and Finn in bear shape had his chin on the top of my pillow. I had some big problems. The first was I was really starting to like these guys. They were bear shifters, and they were some of the nicest individuals I'd ever encountered. How did I reconcile the two in my head?

They were deeply asleep. Did that have to do with what Rylan said earlier about torpor? They slept more in the winter, but not through the whole winter? Was this winter? It was kind of pleasant.

I needed to pee, so I sat up slightly to slide out of the bed. Finn's body shifted, the change going in reverse of what I'd seen Rylan do, to become a human again. He was still in the clothes he'd been in the day before. Maybe they were absorbed and recreated in the process. Or something. His eyes flew open. "Where are you going?"

I pointed to the bathroom. "That okay?"

He rubbed his eyes. "Yes, sorry. I wake up always ready for action. Go, of course."

I almost snapped about needing permission, but I was really tired of having to battle when there wasn't one. Maybe some things could just be simple. I got out of bed, afraid of jarring Rylan, but he never moved.

I took care of my needs, including washing my face, and came back out to find both of them asleep, Finn in his human form this time. I stared at the bed. The spot for me was right there. I shouldn't still be tired. It wasn't like I was a bear. They might need to sleep a lot during the winter months, but I should be fine. It wasn't even that cold.

I climbed back into the bed, and Finn's eyes flew open. He wrapped an arm around me. Not pulling me to him, just holding on. "Sorry. Once every five years we all go through this torpor. We're coming out of it now. It's getting warm, although today, I think, will be cold. That's how you managed to get down onto the planet unbothered. That's how you beat Rylan and the other bears in the chase through the woods. That's how you got in here without me knowing it. We're all off. Once every five years. If the wolves knew, they'd invade. It's a secret."

If it was such a secret, they shouldn't tell me. I was a stranger. They thought I was their mate, and probably that was what mates did, they told secrets. The truth was I'd never tell. "Sleep if you need to. I'm still surprisingly tired myself. Weird. I'm a pretty high energy person."

"You've had a long couple days, and you're hurt." He looked at my forehead. "Pain?"

"Little bit but not like yesterday."

Finn started to move, and it occurred to me he was going to go get that shot. I grabbed his arm. "That medicine gave me weird nightmares. I'd rather have the pain."

He made a low noise in his throat, and then he made it again. His eyes flashed bear then returned to their human look. Finn retook his place in the bed, his arm around my waist again. "I can't think of anything I hate more than you in pain."

"That's. . .sweet." It really was. Even Calvin had been less than concerned when I got injured. We were more like a rub some dirt in it and move on kind of a family.

He smirked. "I can be sweet. Sometimes. To you, I will be. Just don't tell anyone. I made an announcement to the bear population last night that you are our mate. That will put an end to any of your fears."

"What?" I squeaked, trying not to wake Rylan. He still didn't budge. "Are you crazy? I can't be your mate. Not really. I have to go. My brother is in prison." I'd already told Rylan, I might as well go all in and tell Finn. "I have to pay to get him out. That's why I was flying. That's the only thing I'm good at. I can't leave him there. He is the only family I have. Plus, there is the whole we are two different species problem."

His eyes were hooded. "We have excellent hearing. When you screamed last night, Rylan got to you first because he was closest. But Cole and I listened, or at least I assume he did, from where we were. I heard you tell Rylan. I heard you come downstairs and hesitate about leaving too. That second part is an assumption. Then Rylan straight out asked you. Never mind. I'm digressing. Don't worry about your brother. I think we're pretty much the same species."

"Don't worry about my brother? Are you kidding?"

Finn put a hand on my shoulder. "For now, don't worry."

I expected my temper to rise. I should be shoving him away, ranting and raving. But his hand felt nice. I'd gotten used to the sound of Rylan's snores; they were sort of rhythmic. Finn was keeping his voice low and soft. For just then, I wouldn't worry.

I closed my eyes.

I woke up hours later. Rylan wasn't snoring, but he was still there. Finn was gone, and I didn't know where Cole was. I hadn't seen him since he drugged me. My head felt pretty good and. . .

Rylan's body was close to mine. So close, in fact, that I could feel that a certain part of his anatomy was hard. Very hard. I looked over my shoulder at him, and his eyes were only slightly open. He gave me a lazy grin.

"Hi, Jessica."

I swallowed. "Hi, Rylan. Thanks for coming in last night."

"Always will if you need me." He rubbed the back of my neck, and then my shoulders. I sighed. "You smell so good."

That pushed me out of my daze. "I don't think that's possible. I'm wearing the same clothes I was in when I got here, and they're all blood stained. They have to stink by now."

"Hard to tell because your overall scent is so intoxicating. You could probably be bathed in mud and I'd love it. You poor thing. You showered and had to put that back on. Wait here." He got out of the bed, and I got a look at of his very erect cock pushing through a slit in his shorts before he left the room, seemingly unconcerned with it. My mouth went dry. Wow, okay. I wasn't sure at all what to do with that. He'd made no move, applied no pressure, but he was clearly turned on.

Or maybe he just always had an erection first thing in the morning. I sighed. I loathed sex, and I wasn't going to do it with them, particularly since I was leaving. Crazy bears in the woods or not, I was going.

Even if they had been really sweet the night before.

I got out of bed and nearly collided with Cole when I went out in the hall. He grabbed my shoulders, a smile on his face. "Hey there, sorry. You need clothes. I'll get some today. You can come with me, if you want. I go check on the bears that live on our lands. One of them is a seamstress for all of us who live around here." He tugged on his shirt. "She made this. She can dress you."

Heat infused my cheeks. It was one awkward conversation after another. "Cole, I'm not staying. You can't make me clothes. You could get me a ride off the planet or call my people. Or something. But clothes might be a waste."

His eyes darkened, and for the first time, I saw the bear in his eyes. Was he about to shift? He blinked, and the bear vanished. "Sorry about that. I don't like when you say you're leaving. Leaving is a foreign concept to us, to an extent. We don't leave. Female shifters do. They go to their new clan when they mate. But leaving, to a degree, is death. I have to keep reminding both sides of myself that you aren't talking about death."

"Cole. . ." I wasn't even sure what to say.

"I'm getting you clothes." His eyes changed again, and this time, he rushed away from me to stare downstairs from the balcony. "Someone comes."

Finn leaned against the doorway to his office. "Yes. I was counting on it. You don't make an announcement like I did and not anticipate a response. This will be the first of many."

Rylan, still in his boxers, came out of the kitchen. He took a long pull of water. "And eventually, war."

Wait. What?

Cole made a huffing sound. "It was about time anyway."

CHAPTER 4

FINN STALKED TOWARD THE DOOR, pointing at his brother, Rylan. "Go put on some clothes. My nose is never wrong. All screwed up from sleeping too much aside, we have company coming, and it's going to be Mark Karhu. I don't remember the last time anyone saw his clan. I think I was fifty when he came by, had a conversation so private with father that they rushed me out of the house. You were there, remember that Cole?"

Next to me Cole shook his head. "Nope. I don't really have memories from those years. I was still battling the bear, and Mom was pregnant with naked over there. She didn't have a lot of patience for me. I was probably in the woods already."

"Well, this is big. It's got to be about my announcement about Jessica. Karhus coming to see Durojos. It is a day for change for sure."

I leaned against the wall. "Finn, why did you do this? I. . .You can't open yourself up to violence over something that isn't real."

He lifted his head to look at me. "Don't tell me what's

real, Jessica. You are the most real thing I've ever had. I'm not going to let anyone or anything come between what this is. Not even you. Start figuring out how to be fine with being my mate."

"Are you kidding?"

He walked to the front door, calling over his shoulder. "Almost never."

Rylan took the stairs two at a time, grumbling the whole time. "You'd think a bear could just hang out in his underwear. You'd think he'd be able to do that at home. But no, a bear has to have a brother who is in charge of the world. So people just feel free to drop by."

I'd smile if I wasn't so freaked out. Cole banged on the balcony. "I'm going to get my visits done. Whatever is going to happen here won't be good news. I may not be able to attend medically to anyone for a while. Plus, we have to know which of our allies are in bad shape." He touched my cheek. "Chin up, Jessica. We go to war every ten years. That's how frequently some asshat decides that someone else should be in charge. The Durojos have yet to lose. We won't be the first."

I sighed. This was getting really complicated, and I hadn't even decided to stay. "What is a Durojo?"

His eyebrows shot up. "That's us. Our last name. Humans have them too. You're Jessica White. We're Cole, Finn, and Rylan Durojo."

I supposed that was something a person should know about their *mates*. Ugh, I hated that word.

Cole ran down the stairs. "I'll be back." He swung around to look at me. "Sorry, making a mental picture so I can look at sizes. Unless you want to come?"

I didn't. Actually a plan was forming in my mind. With this new arrival of some importance, Finn and Rylan were going to be busy. Cole was leaving. I could run. I'd get away from them and their crazy mate talk—and sweetness at night, and the way that they were already sort of worming their way into my heart—and hide out until I. . .

Truth was, I was sick to death of my own thinking. I was dumb, but I wasn't stupid. They weren't coming for me. My people would leave me here to face my fate. No one got off Planet Bear. If there was any way humans could be returned, it would have happened by now. There was nothing for me there except a job that let me die and my brother, who I was bound to fail.

I wanted to save him. That was all that I wanted.

Cole's expression fell. "Jessica, are you okay?"

"I've never been okay." I swallowed. "I am screwed up. I am going to die in an explosion. There's no one in the universe that loves me. My brother doesn't even care all that much. I love him, but it's not both ways. And you should have a better mate who won't cause you war because she can't shift."

My knees didn't want to work, and I gave up trying to make them. I sank to the ground. Two seconds later, Cole was by my side. He sat next to me.

"Come here." He pulled me into his arms, and I let him hold me there on the floor because I was weak. Because I was so tired of being in my own head. All of this was weird. I knew it. I couldn't explain it.

I leaned my head on his shoulder, but I didn't cry. What were the point of tears anyway?

He rubbed my back, and a fully dressed Rylan sunk down next to us. "Don't you see what happened, Jess?"

I lifted my head to look at him. "What? What happened?"

"You finally found your way home. Of all the places in

the universe, you came to this house. You found where you were supposed to be. That's all."

I laughed. "That's happy ending talk. I don't believe in them."

From the bottom of the stairs, Finn called up. "We do."

"Aren't you with some important bear?"

Finn practically flew up the stairs. He ducked down toward us. "He can wait outside. He can hear us as well as I could hear you. Smelled your tears that you're not shedding, and it's like a gut punch. You're my mate. Everyone else can politely wait outside anytime you need something."

I had enough of being a drama queen. "Okay, let's get to it. Cole, yes, I'll come with you. I was going to run away, but I'm not. Finn, have your meeting. Rylan, what are you going to do?"

He pointed at Finn. "Guard his ass."

Finn rolled his eyes. "From the elderly bear who was a friend of our fathers? Thanks. Jessica, before you go, Mark is rather insistent on meeting you. I can say no."

"Sure, I'll meet him. Why not? I'm meeting bears all over the place. But if this turns out to be what I said and all bears think they want to mate me, I'm going to be pissed."

Cole kissed my cheek. It was a warm, unexpected gift. "Yes, so will we. Trust me. Because no one else gets you."

I straightened my clothes and followed them downstairs and out the front door. The temperature had severely dropped while I'd been inside. Rylan's eyes turned bear. Was it the cold or something else?

Weather seemed like it really played a huge factor in their lives

"I had to see for sure." The shifter called Mark looked like an older gentleman to me, as if he were a top level Union employee. He had thick, gray hair and brown eyes. "I had to make sure you weren't completely different from your father and this wasn't some kind of a trick."

I put my hand on Rylan's back. I wasn't even sure why, but it seemed like he might need me. I leaned into him, and some of his muscles unclenched.

Finn was very still. "I've been leading this world for thirty years. At any time you wanted to know me, to learn who I was, you could have come here. I haven't been hiding. I am available to everyone."

"A bear come seeking help?" Mark laughed. "You know we'd all rather die. No, seriously, you are a good leader. But one hundred years ago, your father advised me to hide my truth from the world. Last night, you threw that on its heel."

The old man walked toward me, and a growl sounded in Rylan's throat. Cole took a step back, placing himself more in front of me. Mark stopped, his gaze moving to Rylan. "You're not quite one hundred yet. I forgot. You were the surprise. Your mother thought she couldn't have any more when no one came for so long after Cole. Then there was you, Rylan. Your fathers were joyous. But you hardly knew them. Sixty years is not enough. Not when so many of them are spent battling the bear. I'll give you some advice from an old man who knew the men who would have made you a man. In case your brothers haven't told you: don't posture. If you mean to fight me, then growl at me. Otherwise, don't."

Rylan's smile was slow and menacing. I let go of his back. I knew that look. I'd seen it on the faces of men all over the galaxy. Aggression mixed with pissed off male. That meant someone was going to be in pain. I hoped it wasn't me.

"If I meant to fight you, you would know. I'm young, but I'm deadly. And, Jessica, don't be afraid. I'd never hurt you. Ever."

Mark nodded. "You don't need to hurt me. I'm an old mated man. I am not after your woman. Not to take her or hurt you. I'm here to help you."

"Mated?" Finn called out. I noted he hadn't interfered with Rylan. What would Finn, who was the leader, have done if Rylan had decided to actually attack Mark? There were a lot of dynamics going on here that I didn't understand.

In fact, now that I looked where Finn stood, they had Mark covered on all sides. What did they think he was going to do to me? Scratch that, I could imagine what they thought. They were bears.

"That's right, Commander." Mark used a title for Finn I hadn't heard before. "Mated. Eighty years ago, a woman appeared on our doorstep. She begged for help. At that point, she was even begging for death. Anything to not stay as she was. She'd been attacked and held captive by the Derby clan. They had hurt her for days and days." He looked abruptly away. "To this day, the fact that she got away awes me. Although I shouldn't be surprised. She has never ceased to awe me. We knew immediately she was our mate. We also knew she was human."

Someone else had mated a human? I looked between them. Finn's expression showed nothing of what he thought. "You came to my father to tell him, and he advised you to hide her. For eighty years?"

I shook my head. "Oh, I doubt it was eighty. I mean, I guess it could be. Was she sixteen when you met her? We don't live that long."

Finn jolted and then covered it. I wondered if anyone else noticed. Mark nodded his head. "We really need to talk. There are things that happen. . .Being mated to us, or maybe it's our planet, or maybe it's something else entirely

—we've never had the means to find out—but she's aging much more slowly. Not on the same timeline as us. But slower. She does seem to be coming to the end of her life now."

Rylan squeezed my hand. "We don't live past our mates, not very long anyway. When our mother was killed during a battle, our fathers followed quickly. They just couldn't do without her."

I swallowed through the choking sensation of grief that might bring me down again. "Then you shouldn't mate me."

Mark gave me a small smile. "You don't know because your brain doesn't work the way that ours do, it doesn't interpret scents you can't consciously identify. But, it has taken you. The mating. You just have to trust it. They can feel it. So can you. Do you want to leave? My Stella kept begging to get off the planet or to die, and then it sort of shifted. A softening to it."

I put my hand over my mouth to keep from snapping out something awful. That's what I did when I was scared. Whatever this hormone or scent or something was having the same effect on me that it was having on them? What in the ever-loving hell was going on here?

Cole smirked. "You like how we smell too." He put out his hand. "Come on, let's go."

Rylan let me go and stepped back. Finn moved around him. "Enough on this porch. You have things to say that I want to listen to. Inside. Rylan, you're with me."

Cole tugged me against him, walking much too slowly for his long legs but clearly wanting to keep pace with me. I shivered. The cold air hit me as my mind started to return to the present and less out of whatever that was.

"You're cold?" He sounded so genuinely surprised I had to check his face to make sure he wasn't joking. He didn't seem to be. "We don't feel the cold all that acutely when we're walking around. It just makes us tired, much more exhausted than we would otherwise be."

He pulled off his shirt, and suddenly, Cole was bare chested. My mouth went dry. He was sculpted like he'd been made by an artist to look that way. Rylan had been, too, now that I thought about it. I'd been able to see his muscles through the tight shirt he'd worn to bed. I'd just been distracted by other alert parts of his anatomy.

"You're going to be freezing."

He shook his head. "I won't even notice." He held out his shirt. "Put it over yours. It'll be twice the warmth. Please."

It really was very sweet. "If you're sure."

"I'm sure."

I took the offering from him and pulled it over my head. The garment was huge on me, but he was right, I was warmer. "Cole, we have a lot of things to talk about. We don't know each other at all, and maybe that's normal for you guys. You just sort it out with your mate, but I have to understand some things and really express to you that I have some important. . .issues."

He nodded. "Like what?"

I made myself stand straight. "War? Can you explain that, please?"

"About every ten years it happens. As far as leadership, a male from our clan is usually in charge. But sometimes we lose. Sometimes the Derby clan—the one that had Mark's wife—leads. Or a group like them. They tend to be hard-core traditionalists. They don't want humans here. They pretty much want us to negate all but the most basic technology. Like we should all be living in caves. Some-how, there is a portion of the population that always supports that crap." He looked away and then finally back to me. "They will come for us. It's okay. They've tried before."

My ears rang. "Cole, before I go any further, I have to tell you that I lash out and yell when I'm frightened or angry. I don't know any other way to respond. I'm trying not to right now. Here in the woods where you are shirtless and sweet."

Half of his mouth went up in a smile. "Okay. You yell. That's okay. No one has ever died from being yelled at. I don't think."

Some of the ringing stopped. Not all of it, but some. "The three of you are going to battle in a war? The three of you against all those people? Because of me?"

"No." He tugged me to him in a hug. "The three of us and thousands more. They have their supporters. We have ours. The people love Finn. They loved my father. Well, one of them. We had four fathers. We don't know which one actually fathered us. It never mattered. Father. Uncle. It's all family here. My one dad was in charge. He was pragmatic but kind."

Cole's skin smelled like springtime. It should feel awkward being on his bare skin, but it didn't. Maybe it was that getting addicted to their scent or mating thing. I didn't care. "I don't get the feeling Finn is pragmatic."

"No, he's optimistic, and he just wants everyone to do the right thing. That's something all three of us have in common. They'll come for us, challenge him, we'll win. Don't fret."

I raised my eyes to look in his. "Didn't your mother die in a battle?"

Sadness moved through his gaze. "She did. Very unexpectedly. It was. . .awful. There are always casualties. No one saw that coming. We won't let anything happen to you. There were lessons to learn. We are different now."

"Cole," I made myself keep talking, "there's something else. I don't like sex. I don't know how any of this can work."

I expected a strong reaction, but he stayed silent so long I wondered if he'd heard me. Maybe this was the thing that would finally make them see this wasn't going to work.

"We don't have sex before mating. We have no real. . .interest in it until then. Please believe me, I can't speak for the other two, but I'm interested now. Um, I had heard that humans engage in intimacy outside of mating. But if you didn't like it, then maybe we can figure out how to like it. Together. Even if that takes some time."

Now it was my time to search for words. "Do you always say the perfect thing?"

He laughed. "No, most of the time I have no idea what the heck to say at all. I leave that to the other two."

We didn't move for a minute. That was okay. I was glad to just stand there with him.

———

Cole visited house after house, checking on the bears. Most of them had received whatever message Finn sent out the night before and knew I was human before I even arrived. They were glad to see Cole. One older female gave him a shirt, which I was both happy and distressed about. I liked looking at him half naked. What did that mean? Was I. . .interested?

I pushed away, wondering. There were too many people to meet, too many stares to ignore. No one was being downright hostile, and I supposed that would have to do. I tried to remember my manners.

On our way to the fifth stop, Cole abruptly quit moving. "We're being trailed. Someone is following us. In their bear form. That's aggressive. I suspect it's. . ." he sniffed the air. "A man named Bronson. He lives in these woods because Finn allows it. Rylan and I would rather he vanish. We've simply not pushed the matter. I am going to deal with him. You." He pointed left. "Walk straight in that direction for two minutes. You'll find a cabin there. It belongs, funnily enough, to Bronson's cousin. They're clan, but they have little to do with each other. It's a long story. Their family is about to die out. They never found mates. Easton used to be a carpenter. Go stay with him. He'll be fine."

I nodded. I wasn't going to argue with Cole, not when he knew what he was doing. Even if what I wanted to do was stay glued to his side. The days I'd spent out here I'd had no idea I was being trailed or even looked for. I was lucky I wasn't dead, dead, dead.

Why hadn't they found their mates? I'd ask him later. Wasn't it just always organic? Like I showed up or they smelled someone on the streets? Was there a main town on this planet? A city? How did it work?

I had to get answers. I hated not knowing things. It didn't take me two minutes, probably because I was running. But I did arrive at the cabin and. . .

Something was wrong. I backed up two steps. I was alive because I trusted my instincts. They'd kept me alive so far. But why I was freaked out here, I couldn't put my finger on instantly. Then it hit me. There was blood on the door. Why was there blood on the door of this wooden cabin?

A roar sounded to my side, and I whirled around to see the second biggest bear I'd ever been around staring at me. He wasn't bigger than Rylan. I didn't know if he'd be larger than Cole or Finn. I'd only seen Finn as a bear lying down.

This one was on two feet, way too close for comfort, and apparently posturing. That was what Mark had called it.

But this didn't look like posturing.

The bear was covered in blood, his light white and brown coat making it obvious. His face had been torn apart. I could only see half of it.

"Hello, Easton." I hoped it was Easton. It was at least a good guess. "You're hurt. I'm so sorry. I'm Jessica. I'm Cole's mate. And Finn and Rylan. We came to check on you, and you're obviously not okay." How much could he understand? "Cole is coming. He can help you."

The bear didn't growl and instead made his way toward me, his head hanging forward in an unusual manner. I thought. Maybe. I mean how much did I know about this? It didn't look like Rylan when he moved. Okay, this was bad. What did I know about bears? I rushed through the little I remembered in my head.

They were deadly. That was pretty much it. He might decide to eat me while I was still alive. I think I preferred the idea of being blown up.

I staggered backward. There were dominance things. Whoever was bigger was in charge. That wasn't going to work out so well for me.

So I did just what I could think of doing. I yelled at the top of my lungs. "Help."

It wasn't brave, but I could be brave and dead or cowardly and alive. Maybe Cole would hear me. They had super sharp hearing, that was for sure.

I ran. I didn't turn around, so doing it backward was awkward and difficult. The thing was I didn't think I should turn my back on a wild, angry, injured animal. The bear had difficulty running, but what it lacked in speed because of its injuries, it certainly made up for in strength and determination. All he had to do was charge. His gaze was on the ground, clearly following my tracks, and I was pretty sure that bears could climb really well.

What in the hell was I going to do?

A growl louder than I'd ever heard, really it was more of a roar, sounded in the air, followed by two more in the distance. What was that? Were the bears from the woods coming? Were they all going to get me? Was this all some elaborate joke? My mates sent me out here to watch me run for my life? No, I dismissed that thought. That was my insecurity talking in my mind when it had no place during this type of crisis.

A huge brown grizzly threw itself in front of me before it rounded on Easton. This wasn't Rylan. The fur was slightly darker. It had to be Cole. He advanced on the other bear. I had never seen bears fight before. I had no idea it would be so silent. But just because it was quiet didn't mean it wasn't gruesome and awful. I backed up significantly, right into another bear. Rylan.

"Hi." My voice shook, but when the giant bear picked me up, I climbed onto his back without fear. In fact, I buried my face into fur.

A low growl stopped everyone from moving. Finn in his bear form, with an older bear behind him, made his way to the scene. Cole stepped away just in time for Finn to deliver the killing blow to Easton.

Just like that, it was done. The only thing I could hear was my own heart in my ears. I pushed my head down on Rylan. I was just going to stay like this until I could think again.

CHAPTER 5

I STARED at the water someone set down in front of me and tried to pull myself together. A bear had almost killed me.

Finn came into my view, sitting on the coffee table and ducking his head down until he caught my gaze. I blinked. Did he need something? In the time since I'd arrived, I'd been nothing but trouble to them.

"I'm always an incredible hassle to have around. This time I was on a path I didn't intend to stray from. Sometimes, shiny objects distracted me, but when I got onto *Goldie,* I swore that I would work my hardest, do everything right, and then get my brother out of jail. Then I'd find a quiet terraformed planet somewhere where I could keep to myself and cause no trouble."

Finn scrunched up his face, and across the room, Rylan made a bear noise I couldn't decipher. He hadn't shifted back yet. I wasn't sure where Cole was, and Mark had left. I thought. Distantly, I'd been listening to things people said.

"You're talking about the ship you were in when the wolves shot you? Goldie. That was her name. That's right." He took my hand in his. "You had a scare. That's for sure.

Did you see how his head sort of bobbed the wrong way? That was an indication of neurological trouble. The way Cole easily took him down and I killed him? That meant Easton was all but dead before I ever got there. Unfortunately, he could still have hurt you. Or worse." A frown formed between his eyes. "Someone hurt him. Cole is determining whom. That's why he wasn't okay. He was already pretty much gone. The quiet Easton I grew up knowing would never have harmed you."

I put my hand on his knee. "Are you okay?"

"Yes, of course." He shook his head. "Why?"

"You had to kill him because I'm a weak human on a planet of very big bears."

Finn leaned forward. "You're my mate."

"Was that supposed to explain why you're, of course, okay? Killing is hard. Period."

He took my hand in his. "Not when it comes to protecting what's mine." A growl across the room made him smile. "Ours." He looked over my shoulder. "Go run it off until the bear leaves. Or shift back."

Rylan made a noise that must have been a harrumph and walked toward the back door. He pushed on the handle, and it opened. Then he sort of slumped off into the woods. Finn rolled his eyes. "Two more years and he'll shift when he wants to and not shift when he doesn't."

He got up and went to close the door.

I took a sip of the water. "Did you get what you wanted from Mark?"

Saying his name made me stop and think. Was his name really Mark? Was Finn really Finn? Our translator devices made us understand each other. What did they hear when I said Jessica? They were probably not Finn and Mark. They were something in their own language.

Finn sat back down. He looked tired. Why did I think that? I wasn't sure. "The weather making you sleepy?"

He answered the first question instead of the second. "I did. He had some things to say. Just basically about the past. My father thinking that it would tear apart the fabric of our society. That there are minimal things that we have done to appease those people over the years and giving up the no human rule would push them too far. They'd attack until they killed themselves." He shook his head. "I think I have a mate that I'm not going to hide or ask her to hide. They can get over themselves, or I'm fine with them fighting themselves to death."

Well, he had already said he didn't mind killing for me. It was such an odd thing to hear. I scooted forward on the couch until our knees touched. I wanted to touch him. It was just on a long list of things I couldn't seem to bring myself to question.

"Maybe no one has to die. Maybe you could talk about it."

He joined our hands together. "If such a thing were possible, it would be done. My only objective has been to continue to help us all thrive. We do. Commerce. Land. Balanced with our inherent need to just be left alone. For the most part, anyway. The Derbys are a problem and those like them. I've left them to their own distressing existences. To their own lives." He raised his gaze to mine. "Maybe that was a mistake. I am not good at talking to people, like Cole. Even Rylan. . ."

I squeezed his knee. "I'm new. I can't have a grasp of all of these things, but you're dominant, yes? To them? Is it just age? Size?"

He smirked. "It's many things. They're incredible males. Either one of them could lead. But, yes, I am.

Slightly. Miniscule amount and basically with their consent. We've never challenged each other."

"Okay, then don't overthink it. Assume they'd take it from you if you weren't the best. Assume you haven't done anything wrong. Go from there. What's next? What would you tell someone to do in your position?"

His nostrils flared. "Protect what is yours. Make them change to suit what is. One quarter of our people never find their mates. They live their life without. . ." His voice trailed off. What word was he looking for? I knew Cole said they didn't have sex. But I didn't think that was the word he sought. "Without." He sighed. "Maybe their mates are above." He pointed toward the sky. "Distances away that can only be found on a spaceship."

"Is there anything I can do to help you?" Probably there wasn't. So far, I'd been nothing but burdensome.

He shook his head. "You are right, Jessica. I am tired."

"Well." I took his hand. "I could tuck you in."

"Could you stay? Just lie down with me. Never mind, too soon. I'm still riding the thinking you were dead thing. I felt your fear, I smelled it. I shifted. I don't remember the last time it just happened like that. Then. . .I don't know. I know I killed him. That's it. And you were okay. That I knew."

He was all over the place. I rose. "Come on. Sure, I'll lie down." Right then, my stomach growled. "Can you wait ten minutes?"

His smile was huge. "My turn to feed you."

Feeding me apparently meant sitting on his lap with that porridge in front of me. I drew the line on letting him spoon it into my mouth.

"Females from here allow their men to feed them. It's an honor."

I sighed. "I'm sitting on your lap. That's about as far as I can go in this. There has to be a line I don't cross and still be able live with myself. Being fed when I am still capable of feeding myself? It's too far."

He leaned his head on my shoulder. "Okay. Feed yourself."

I rolled my eyes. "I was going to whether you gave me permission to or not."

"I know. That's sort of amazing. Don't stop doing that."

There he was, acting like I needed permission to do what I was going to do. I was seeing a trend happening here. That was fine. He was warm. I shifted on his lap and suddenly became aware of something else—he was hard.

Heat traveled up my body all at once. My heart rate kicked up a notch. "Are you, ah, hungry?"

"I am not." He stroked a hand down my back. "You eat. You're still recovering. I actually don't eat all that much. More like a big meal that lasts me a long time."

I ate the rest of my porridge and set the bowl aside. "Thank you. That was delicious. I have to eat a lot. Three times a day. Sometimes snacks."

"We haven't fed you enough. That's unacceptable that we've been negligent. It will get better."

"I can feed myself." Sometimes, I'd fed my brother and myself. My good mood fled. Calvin. In jail. I sighed. If I stayed here, his whole life was in that jail.

Finn stroked my back. "What distresses you?"

"My brother. I thought about him, and yeah." I got off his lap, picked up my bowl, and went to the sink.

Finn rose. "Trust me. He is our clan. Arrangements will be made. He will not be in jail."

"How?" I turned to face him, and his arms came around me.

"I have my ways," he whispered in my ear. "Trust me."

Cole came through the door then, yawning. "It wasn't Bronson. It seems he didn't lie. He wanted to check out the human, to quote him, and that's all he was doing. His scent is not on the scene, and he mourns his clan mate. No, I smell Derby there. This was purposeful, and it couldn't be because of Jessica. Too quick. They came before this. Probably stayed just enough away and waited until we were distracted."

Rylan leaned in the doorway. "They need to sleep, the same as we do. Or don't. I can resist it."

Finn shook his head. "You can't even control your shift yet."

"No, that's true. But my bear doesn't need to sleep as much as I seem to as a human. Let me go bear. Let me find them. Let me end them. They attacked a bear on our land. That bear tried to hurt my mate." His voice lowered. He'd just shifted back. He was going to do it again so soon?

Cole touched Rylan's arm and looked at Finn. This was what leadership was. They would defer to him. They trusted him.

He nodded at Rylan. "If you say you can, you can. Be back by tomorrow night. You need to do something nice for our mate tomorrow night. Don't stand her up."

Rylan's mouth fell open. "I would never disappoint her."

"I know. So make sure your bear knows too. You're back. Tomorrow night."

Cole rubbed his eyes as Rylan ran out the door. "I'm going to sleep. Good luck, Rylan. You got this, brother. I will get you some clothes, Jessica, tomorrow. I promise."

"You can put on one of my shirts." Finn led me toward the stairs. "Trust me on your brother."

I sighed. "I have a hard time trusting anyone."

Thinking of that, if we were going upstairs to lie down, I had to tell him what I'd told Cole. "Finn," I swallowed. "This is so uncomfortable. I can't believe I'm having to say it twice, let alone once. I don't like sex."

I did, however, like sitting on his lap. I liked Cole's bare chest. And I liked seeing Rylan hard. What was the matter with me?

Finn stopped moving. We were halfway up the stairs. "Well, that might be because you were doing it with the wrong people. Don't worry. We can get to that. Despite your short lifespan, we're not in a hurry. And I don't know if either Cole or Rylan told you—whichever one you had this discussion with—but we really get turned on by your arousal as much as anything else. Believe me, I'm. . .aware of you in a way I've never been before. It's. . .stimulating. But what will really get me off, I think that's the way to put it, is when you want it. I'll smell your arousal, and then I'll know."

I swallowed. "What if I never get that way?"

"Trust me."

He was always saying that. It seemed the majority of his planet trusted him. So why couldn't I? "What makes me nervous, Finn, is how fast this happened. Things that blow up quickly deflate that way too."

His face fell for a second before he touched the side of my face. "This is forever. The second we scented you, you became as essential as air."

It was quiet in his room. The ceiling fan whooshing slightly over our heads was the only sound. Finn wasn't sleeping. He linked our fingers together. "Tell me what scared you last night. When Rylan came. I was in bear form. I can't really remember if I heard or not."

"Bad dreams. My brother. Things exploding. I'm sorry. I'm usually quiet. I learned to be in the orphanage."

He sat up on his elbow. "I'm not understanding what you said. It's not translating."

"Orphanage?"

Finn shook his head, a piece of his brown hair falling in his eyes. I reached out to push it away. "A place where people who don't have parents or anyone to take care of them are sent to live. In this case, it wasn't a nice location. They used us for labor and hurt us all the time."

He was so still and quiet I wondered if he'd fallen asleep. "Let me see if I get this straight. When children don't have homes or family to take them, they are brought somewhere to live and do labor?"

"In this particular case, yes." I rolled away from him, already regretting bringing it up. "We were taken by the authorities when they arrested my uncle. When he finally bought his way out of jail, he came back for us. It wasn't that big of a deal."

Finn touched my shoulder, gently. "You say that, and yet your scent tells a different story."

"What does it say?" I cut him off before he could answer. "It's everything I can do not to start lashing out at you. I told Cole earlier, that's my go-to response for nearly everything. That's how I survive. Whatever is happening between us, it is fundamentally changing me. I couldn't have stopped myself two days ago."

Finn rolled over on his stomach and tugged me to him so I was on my side against him. "Nothing about you has fundamentally changed. Not a thing. Maybe you're just. . .breathing for the first time ever. I hate that my love was in some. . .place. . .without family."

"I had my brother. I took care of him."

He growled, deep in his throat. "Someone should have taken care of you. Were you harmed?"

"Yes." But I didn't want to talk about it, not more than that. They were memories, buried so far inside of me that I never let them rise. The beatings. The tauntings. The starvation. I'd never been violated sexually, but that was just because I was lucky.

He didn't push. Instead, he kept stroking his hand from the top of my head down my back. It was a relaxing feeling. "Here, that would never happen. If someone is killed or an entire clan dies, a neighbor or another clan takes them in. Even the Derbys, they would do this. It is how we are. No child would grow up without family. Our child would never be alone."

I sucked in my breath. Our child? That was just another thing that should be making me run away and wasn't. I wasn't ready to see myself as a mother, but I didn't want to flee because he'd said that aloud. "Humans have one mother, one father. Sometimes a step mother or father. But no clans. Who would take in our child? Let's say I die having that child."

This time it was his turn to suck in his breath. "That would not happen. Cole would not allow it."

"This is hypothetical scenario time. Say I die. Who takes care of this child since you three will want to die too, right? That's how it'll work."

He smoothed my hair again. "The child would go live with cousins of ours or some of our friends. The child would have more people to love it than you can possibly imagine. Lovely woman. Don't worry. The fading isn't all at once. It's over time, and then the person just goes. That wouldn't happen until the baby was secured."

I liked that answer. "Okay." I had to remember he was tired. "You need to sleep."

"Yes, but I'm fine. I smell tiredness on you. It increases as you are with me. I wonder if you are somehow being affected by our need to rest during the cold." He turned his head slightly. "Rylan wasn't a baby. But we raised him these years, sort of. Brotherly raising. He is a strong bear, and soon he will be totally in control."

I didn't really understand. "You've said that before. Battle the bear."

"From about age twenty until age one hundred, there is a rolling around between bear and man. It isn't just one at that point. Rylan has to win. And he is. There are years where the man spends more time as a bear than a man."

So it was like shifter puberty. Okay. I could understand that. "Got it. You start out like human babies, and the shifting comes at twenty?"

"You know it's coming, but it still scares the heck out of you." His smile was big, toothy. He yawned.

"Finn." I brought his knuckles to my mouth. "Sleep."

He nodded. "This is what I wanted. When I thought about what we didn't have, what we might not have since so many of our people don't, what I wanted was to have someone to talk to in the dark. Quiet conversation. Maybe about nothing important but that someone who would listen to me ramble, to not make sense when exhaustion came."

I snorted. "I'm not exactly known for my great conversation skills."

"I love how you talk." He rolled onto his back. Finn was clearly having trouble settling. He was adorable, and I needed to kiss him more than anything else in the world. Right then.

I didn't overthink it, I simply pressed my mouth to his, and my body came alive. My breasts ached, my nipples poking out painfully. He moaned against my mouth before he pulled back just slightly.

"Your scent." He closed his eyes. "How it moves through me. I can't. . ."

I kissed him again, and he soon tugged me even closer. Finn was harder than before. His mouth pressed to mine, again and again. He wasn't sure what he was doing. He kept starting and stopping before he found his rhythm, but, wow, I got lost in his enthusiasm.

I'd never felt like this. Kissing had been awkward the few times I'd done it, as though I was being judged on my skill level. Finn just seemed to want me, however it went. I wrapped my arms around his neck, and I held on.

My tongue pushed through his lips, and soon he got what I wanted from him. His own met mine. We moaned together. I wanted to be closer to him, so much closer.

I tugged at his shirt. I'd not wanted this hours before, and now I couldn't have enough. Not nearly. Maybe not ever. This mating. I wouldn't resist it. How could I? We were soon naked, and I hardly remembered getting that way. He pulled back, his gaze on my body.

"You're so much more than I ever thought you could be. I don't know how to tell you, mate. I don't know how to make you see, make you understand."

I breathed in slowly. "Finn, I can't scent you, but I can feel you." I put my hand over his heart. "I can feel it beat the same way you can feel mine."

He nodded. Maybe we would finally understand each other. Sort of. He brought my palm to his mouth and kissed it. "I wish to bring you pleasure, my mate. I don't know how, and I don't want to be another reason you don't wish to do this."

Wow, I had really stressed him out. I hadn't even considered the pressure what I told him must have brought.

"Kiss me. I want you, so much. Everywhere. I'm sorry if you've worried. I. . ."

His mouth took possession of mine, and his hands were all over my body. I loved every touch. I ran my hands over his chest, feeling his muscles, the definition, the way his pulse jumped beneath my fingertips.

The way it felt when his body came over mine. I spread my legs, feeling his hard cock close to it as he brushed against me. I dropped my hand, reaching for his cock, and stroking it. Once. Twice. It grew in my hand. He moaned.

"Such pleasure that you give me, mate. I had no idea. How have I done without you?"

I took his hand. Sometimes in the middle of the night, alone with no one to hear, I had touched myself. There were ways I could bring myself some pleasure. I ached for more, but it had done. Now, I showed him where I wanted to be touched, the spot that I liked. Before I'd lost interest in it altogether.

Finn quickly followed my unspoken direction. His breathing picked up. "Yes, show me. I want to know all of you."

I was getting wet, and my hips arched off the bed. This had never happened to me before, not like it was now.

"Jessica," his voice shook, "I want to be deep inside of you."

I nodded, spreading my legs. "Please. Do it." This had been the worst part of it the last time I'd done this. But everything about our encounter felt like I'd never done it before.

Finn nodded. He pushed inside of me. I stretched to fit him, and he waited, like he understood I needed a minute before I could proceed. I touched the side of his face, running my fingers over his whiskers. "Take me, please."

"Oh but, Jessica, I think it is you who has me."

He pressed deeper inside of me and then pulled out. Some things were natural. Finn had never done this before, but he certainly knew what he was doing. My body was on fire. Wanting, needing, oh yes, this was what I had been waiting for.

Over and over, we joined until I was panting, crying out, begging for more. I didn't know what I needed exactly, but I knew it could only come from Finn. He had to give it to me. He pressed down between us, right where I had shown him. I exploded and seconds later so did Finn. He called out my name. I wasn't sure if there wasn't a little bit of growl in how he said it. I loved the sound. I closed my eyes. The pleasure was too much. All I could do was ride the wave.

I opened my eyes sometime later, snuggled against Finn. He held me tight against him. His eyes were closed, and he breathed deeply. Finn was clearly asleep. Out cold. The room was chilly and now that the amazing moments were over, I could feel it. I eased out of bed, not wanting to disturb him, and grabbed another blanket I saw draped over a chair. I wrapped both of us in it and snuggled back against his side.

Tomorrow, I would sort things out. I just had to sleep. I didn't want to be cold anymore, not when there was so much warmth here to be found.

CHAPTER 6

I DIDN'T KNOW if I dreamed. At some point, the bed dipped, and Cole must have joined us. I didn't open my eyes. I just knew it was he who had nestled in behind me. The world faded again. It was my stomach that woke me. It grumbled, needing food. Whatever it was that was changing me, making me feel okay about what should have been lunacy, hadn't altered my need to eat.

The bears might not need to eat regularly, but I did.

They both lay still while light came through the windows. I guessed it was mid-morning. I scooted down the center of the bed as to not wake either of them and padded my way to Finn's drawers. I simply couldn't continue to go along in the clothes I'd been wearing for so long. I grabbed Finn's shirt and put it on. If he didn't like it, I guessed I'd get to see his temper for the first time.

Cole's eyes opened, and he extended his hand to me. "Jessica, come back. The bed is cold without you."

He wasn't really awake. Cole dropped his hand and rolled over. They were back-to-back now, as though all I needed to do was crawl back in. I might have considered it if my stomach didn't beg me to fill it. I'd come back after I ate.

I went downstairs. The house was cold, the way the bedroom had been. I looked around. When I'd headed up the night before, I hadn't thought it at all chilly. Was it possible it wasn't actually any different in temperature right now? Maybe I was just being sensitive to it now. In any case, I was cold in Finn's t-shirt that fell past my knees. I hated even opening the fridge, but I stood in front of it, trying to decide what to eat. Since I'd been here, it had been only the one salmon dish and the porridge. I was going to have to do better than that.

Eggs, it seemed, like salmon, looked very similar, and I soon discovered some other things that seemed familiar. I stumbled through the kitchen and managed to cook myself some food. Eggs and something that reminded me of bacon. I was ravenously hungry. Cole's footsteps behind me alerted me that I wasn't alone.

He sat down in the chair next to me. All of the furniture in this house was huge, and yet with Cole, it looked regular sized. I broke the bacon in half and put it near his mouth. He took a bite and grinned. "I'm the one supposed to be feeding you."

I took my own bite of the other half of the bacon. "Did your mother seriously take all of her meals with someone else feeding it to her?"

"Not every meal." He shook his head. "My fathers were so busy. There were times it was just her here with us. She fed herself then. But if they were here? Yes, they fed her. They loved it. They'd be utterly upset with us that we're not. It seems sort of obvious though that you'd rather we not, so I guess we'll just do things very differently in our relationship."

I finished eating. "That was good."

I closed my eyes, leaning against the chair. "This chair is too big for me. I'm not complaining. Just stating a fact. Two of me could fit in this chair."

"Well, when I go for the clothes I can. . ." His voice trailed off. "Shifters are coming. Four of them just crossed into our territory. I can smell them. Three of them are friends. The fourth turns sides. Back and forth. There's nothing I hate more. Pick a side. Finn will. . ."

The aforementioned brother rushed into the room. He was fully dressed, and rather than take the stairs, he leaped over the balcony onto the ground. I gasped. I'd never seen any of them do that before. Apparently, their extra abilities extended to when they weren't just bears.

"Do me a favor." Cole rose. He had something that looked like a medical swabbing device in his hand. "Let me get a sample from your cheek? Okay?"

I blinked. "For what?"

"Hurry up. I want her not visible when they get here. They can smell her, that's fine. Our scent is all over her. That's a good thing. I don't want her here for them to see. Not with McDermott coming with them."

Cole nodded. He pushed the device in my mouth and swabbed. I wanted to know why, but Finn's composure held my attention across the room. He was tense. Whoever this McDermott shifter was, he was important.

They didn't hold him in high regard. Cole took my arm, grabbed a blanket off the couch, and hustled me into what I thought of as Finn's office space. It was where he kept disappearing. Computers and screens lined the walls. Dots flashed on those areas and there was a general buzzing noise that I couldn't hear in the rest of the house. Cole took the swab device he used on me, shoved it into a hole in one of the machines, and then punched in some buttons.

"I'm going to close you in here. This particular space seals off from the rest of the house. You can let yourself out. Put your hand on that button and hold it down for a solid five seconds. It will unlock. But I'd rather you waited in here until we came to get you."

This was all happening really fast. "Cole. . ."

He kissed me. "Easton was sick. He attacked you because he was already pretty much dead. This guy coming, we're pretty sure he reports on us to the Derbys. We're not hiding you, but I don't want him to have any information other than yes he smelled a human in the house. I don't want him to be able to describe you. What you look like or how tall you are. He's not to be trusted around my mate. There's a bathroom right in that section. Finn has a bed in the corner that pulls down from the wall. There are books."

I sighed. "My translator isn't going to work on books. I can only hear what you're saying in my language, not read it."

He kissed my cheek and shoved the blanket into my arms. "Sorry. This is safety."

And just like that, Cole shut me in Finn's office. Disappointment settled on my shoulders like gravity suddenly weighed more. Or something. They could have asked me. We were going to talk about this at length when I got out of this room. My gaze flew to the door Cole had closed. There were scratch marks all over it. I didn't know scratch marks by sight like some kind of expert tracker, but I would wager it was a pretty good guess that those were bear marks. Someone had been trapped in here before and clearly not wanted to be.

I ran my hands over the marks. How long had they left whoever that was in here? I wrapped myself in the blanket and wandered the room. This space was so different than anywhere else in the house. Technology hadn't seemed like it was much of a factor here. The guys seemed like they lived in practically ancient times. Except in here. This was pretty advanced stuff.

I knew spaceships, and that was about it. Still, a lot of this looked like space monitoring devices. I didn't know, and I didn't want to start pushing buttons randomly. Who knew what he controlled in here? I could launch a missile.

Of course, if any of those wolves happened to be flying around up there, maybe I would shoot them down. Just because they seemed to like to fire on people for no reason in particular.

I took the blanket, pulled down Finn's bed, and lay down. The not reading was going to be a problem. I hadn't even considered it. I sighed. This was only one of what I was sure would be a million issues. I had nothing to do here. The bears didn't even travel through space. They weren't going to need me to deliver supplies. I couldn't just lie around and be fed.

Of course, last night had been the greatest night of my life. I didn't know I could feel that way. Then to wake up between Cole and Finn, all warm and relaxed, only added to the sensation.

I chewed on my fingernail. Where was Rylan? Was he okay? My head was so full with worry.

The door opened and closed as Rylan ducked into the room. He grinned at me. "Mission accomplished."

I sat up straight. "You got the guy who hurt Easton?"

"I did. I mean, yes. My bear self did." He kicked off his

shoes. "And Finn was smart as usual, telling me that I had to get back for you. My bear ran. I hate this room, but I'd rather be in here with you than out there listening to everyone say nothing and somehow mean everything at the same time. I don't do politicking. Let them come. I'll kill them."

I slid over, and he lay down next to me. "I was just starting to worry about you."

"I'm strong and lethal. Don't ever worry about me." He took a deep breath. "You smell like family now. It's intoxicating. The Durojo scent is all over you, but it's not enough. Take your shirt off."

I should have been either stunned, mad, or embarrassed by that statement. I was none of those things. I yanked Finn's shirt over my head and threw it to the side, leaving me totally naked in front of Rylan. That was okay. I'd been nude in front of his brothers, and there was just something about all three of them.

The mating had certainly made me comfortable around them. That was for sure.

He yanked his own shirt off and, like I couldn't do it myself, pushed it down over my head until it fell on me. He nodded. "There. Now you'll smell like me too. Then it'll be perfect."

Rylan was the broadest of all of them in his shoulders. I thought he might have been just slightly shorter than Cole, which still made him tall as all heck. I crooked my finger. "I hear there's a bathroom back there. I need a shower. Give me five minutes. Then join me."

His eyebrows shot up. "Yes."

I steamed up the bathroom getting the water hot. I quickly washed my hair and body. If this went well, I might not actually spend any time getting clean as much as getting to stand in the hot water with Rylan. The shower door flung open. My five minutes was up.

He raised his eyebrows slowly. "You want me. I can smell it."

"Well, let's say you couldn't smell it. Your first hint would have been that I took off my shirt, and the second would be that I invited you into the shower with me."

His eyes turned bear. I touched his cheek. "Can you hold the bear off?"

"He's not coming out here right now." He had taken his clothes off before he came in the bathroom, and my gaze went to his cock. He was huge.

I had been totally disinterested in sex, and now I was a maniac wanting it. "Can I touch you?"

"Anywhere you want."

I took his hand, tugging him under the spray with me. It was warm but not too hot. When he was sufficiently wet, I grasped onto his cock and stroked him, hard. He closed his eyes. "Jessica."

"Rylan." I kissed his chest. "I asked if I could touch you." I caressed him from balls to tip, and he moaned. I loved the sound.

He smirked at me. "I thought you meant my chest. Maybe my ass."

"My translator just said ass. I think that's hysterical." I kissed his chin.

He breathed in, his hands roaming my body, up and down my arms, my back. "Is that a bad word in your language?"

I never answered him. Instead, we got lost in kissing. I had been right about the shower being the perfect place to do it. With a group outside in the house, doing whatever they were doing, we were cocooned in this bathroom.

Or at least I could pretend we were. The thought somewhat dampened my enthusiasm. Could all the people out there hear us? "Are we on display in the sense that they are all listening to us?"

"No." He kissed my neck. "They can't hear anything back here. My grandfather designed this area of the house to be scent proof and sound proof. I would never, ever let you be exposed like that." He hoisted me up. "Enough of this shower. I want you out of it. I don't know what I'm doing, and I'm going to make a fool of myself in here."

At least he hadn't heard my speech about not liking sex. Seconds later, I was in a towel and over his shoulder. I squealed. It was a funny noise for me to make. I couldn't say I'd ever done it before. He laid me down on the bed, and his grin was huge.

"You're my mate. You fell from the sky, and you found your way home to me. Blows my mind."

I winced. "I did a little more than fall from the sky."

"I can't think of you crashing. Makes me want to hurt something, and I've got no one to take that out on. So I'll just repress that and concentrate on your beautiful body. You'll tell me what I'm doing right and wrong. I'll learn, fast."

I blinked. Laughter threatened and I knew that was absolutely the wrong thing to do at this moment. "Okay. We'll do that."

He nodded. It must have been the affirmation he needed because then he was on top of me. He used his elbows to keep his full weight away. But, he was so close I could feel his heat and his weight like a barrier between me and just everything else that ever was.

Rylan had told me more than once that he was deadly. But not to me. I could feel that truth, deep inside.

We kissed, and the noises he made practically drove me to distraction. They were somewhere between growls and moans, sometimes alternating, and just from kissing me, he got harder and harder. He'd wanted instruction. He could have it.

I took his hand and put it on my breast. Usually, I didn't find them to be particularly sensitive. It was very whatever when my own hand touched them. But Rylan's callused fingers were a different thing altogether. He squeezed my nipple, and I cried out. I craved him.

Rylan took my nipple into his mouth and sucked. I closed my eyes and let him worship me. Why not? If this all just turned out to be a respite before I blew up, then I was going to love every damn second of it. I ran my hands through the back of his thick hair. He sucked harder, driving his hips into the bed. His breathing sped up.

If he was going to lose it. I wanted him to do it deep inside of me, not anywhere else.

"Rylan," I opened my eyes. "Let's slow down." I tried to breathe. "So you can be inside of me. Do you want that? To be joined?"

He nodded. "Yes."

Rylan kissed down my body from my breasts all the way until he was at my pussy. "I. . ." He slapped his forehead. "I'm really being overwhelmed."

"Lose it inside of me."

He nodded again, and I grabbed on to his shoulders, tugging him to me. I kissed him slowly before I rolled over onto my stomach. "From behind."

Rylan adjusted himself until he could push deep inside of me from that angle. We both cried out. I held on to the handles on the top of the bed. They didn't give me much to brace myself with, but it was better than nothing.

"This was how I wanted you. This was it." He breathed in my ear.

"I know." I just did. "Take me, Rylan."

My muscles had to stretch to accommodate him. This was a new position to me and the penetration was different. At first, I wasn't at all sure that I liked it. Oh, there was nothing that Rylan could do to me that I wouldn't find hot, but the movement took a minute for me to adjust to. And then he hit my spot.

It wasn't even something I knew I had. Oh, I'd heard about the darn thing in books and from the way other women giggled about it, but I hadn't known. Not really. Until he rubbed against the area. This was something else entirely. My clit had taken time to warm up, like every pass over it brought more and more pleasure. That had been incredible. But this was sudden and it was all encompassing. I could even see how it might sometimes be too much. Only it was exactly what I needed.

I lost hold of the headboard, and Rylan held me instead. Plunging in and out of my body until I quivered with need. My orgasm wasn't going to be far away. It was coming and it was arriving hard.

"Rylan." I had to speak his name. I couldn't see him, but I needed him to hear me. "Oh, Rylan."

He shuddered behind me. I could feel his forehead on my back, his warm breath hitting my skin. "Jessica, this is so much. I can't. . ."

He didn't have to say anything. I understood. And with a jerk of his hips, he sent me over the edge. I came on a low moan before my body trembled. I wasn't sure I could stop if I wanted to. Rylan wasn't done. It took another minute for his completion, but that was okay. Every second he was inside of me was heaven. I'd never, ever get enough.

I didn't let myself fall asleep naked. There was too much risk that that door was going to open. So, even though I hadn't worried about it when Rylan and I had been having sex, I did when it was over. I put his t-shirt back on and climbed into the bed. He lay on his side, watching me.

"I usually hate this space." He yawned while he covered us both up. "Hate it. But I like it now. You changed my feeling of these rooms."

"Why do you hate it? And why do you use blankets at all if you never feel cold?"

He kissed my cheek. "Because this is the room where I got locked in while my mother was killed. She locked me in here. We didn't have the way to get out back then. If you were locked in, this is where you stayed until someone let you out. I clawed and clawed at the door. I couldn't smell anything. Couldn't hear it. But I knew. She was dying. I could have helped her."

I sighed. There was sadness in his eyes, and I knew regret. "You were young, yes? Still battling the bear? And it was harder then?"

He side-eyed me. "Yes. To this day, I still believe I could have helped her. I'm physically stronger than Finn and Cole. I know that's weird. Should make me dominant, but my bear likes listening to Finn's. I like to attack, I think. To fight. Finn is more cautious. That's why he wins more. He waits. He plots. Even shifted, that's what he's like. I could have helped her." He yawned again. "Sorry, it's cold out. You must know by now more about that. The blanket? It isn't that we can't feel the cold. We just aren't bothered by it. It does feel better to be covered. We could sleep through the cold with no blanket. It would just kind of suck."

I lifted my head. "So when Cole gave me his shirt and said he couldn't feel the cold out there. . ."

"He was lying."

I laughed. "Got it."

"Don't worry if I doze off. If someone other than Finn or Cole were to figure out we were back here and come, I'd wake instantly."

I put my head on his arm. "I trust you, Rylan."

He shuddered, and then he kissed me so softly. I almost cried from the gentleness of it. "I'll never let you down, Jessica. I. . .I'm going to pull it together with the bear."

"What?" I didn't really understand what he said? "Translation issue?"

"I am going to get control of the shifting."

"Isn't that supposed to happen in about two years?" Was I really not getting what they were telling me?

Rylan frowned. "I'm going to get ahead of it early. I can't have you worrying that you have a mate that might lose it. That won't be good for the development of your relationship with me."

Oh, I suddenly got it. "Rylan, I wasn't worried about that at all. I have so many things to get through in my head. You seem perfect to me. Don't fret." I patted him. Finn did the same thing when he was tired. He rambled. "You're overdue to let the cold take you. I'll watch out for you."

"Thanks." He didn't sound like he was kidding. He legitimately seemed to like that I said I would watch out for him. Not that I could take on a bear, but some idiot in his non-shifted form would find I could hold my own in a fight.

Rylan's breathing changed. Once second he was awake, the next he was asleep. I was wide awake. I listened to him breathe and the whooshing of the computers in the background.

The tears that came startled me. I hadn't known I was

about to cry, and suddenly I was sobbing. Rylan's eyes flew open. "What's the matter? Did I do something?"

"No." I wiped them away. "Sorry. Please don't worry about me. I'm just overwhelmed, and there's nothing you can do about it. I'm always causing problems. Pretty much since birth. I bring trouble. I'm hiding in a room while they figure out war over me out there. You came in to guard me. Don't give me any more of that ridiculous story about not wanting to do politics. My brother. . ." I didn't finish that thought. Finn asked me to trust him. I'd have to see what was happening on that. "I can't spend my life locked in this room every time someone comes, and it's only been twenty-four hours, so I just need to shut up. I never cry, but I keep crying here."

He made a sound deep in his throat that sounded like a whimper and drew me even closer to him. He smelled warm and spicy, like cinnamon and something else. "What's happening to you? It's happening to all of us. That's part of the mating. It. . .opens us up. Brings things out. My inability to protect my mother isn't something I ever talk about. But boom, I just did. Finn should never have just announced your presence the way he did. It's the mating. He can't hide what he loves. The idea that Mark and others did blows my mind. How did they manage? I. . ." His voice fell off. "This is all going to be okay. I told you before. You came home. That has to feel weird after so much time, your whole life, not being where you belonged."

I had to tell him the truth. "I don't believe in fate or 'supposed to.' This happened. But I don't know that there is any rhyme or reason for it."

"That makes me sad." He kissed my forehead, hard. "But I'll believe enough for the both of us."

CHAPTER 7

I WOKE UP ALONE. I didn't remember falling asleep, but the heating blankets that were my bear shifters seemed to do that to me. Also, whatever was happening to them with the not-quite-hibernating-but-still-sleeping-a-lot thing was taking its toll on me as well. I didn't wake up when Rylan left, whenever that had been, but the dinging from the machine Cole had put my sample into did wake me up. It sounded a lot like the alarms they used to have in the orphanage. *Ding*. I'd jump out of my skin. It seemed I still did.

I walked over to it just as Cole came through the open door. "Sorry, I hoped to get in here before it did that."

"What is it doing? Analyzing me?"

He put his arm around me and pulled me into a hug. "Yes. Letting me see your DNA. I do a lot more than just visit neighbors. I'm a scientist. I promise you, I know what I'm doing. Sort of." He winked at me. "You have dark circles under your eyes. You just woke up. Do you need more food? Exactly how many calories per day should you be getting as a human? You know what? Don't tell me. People rarely know what they need to be doing to take care of themselves. I'll look it up."

"I feel really tired. I can't explain it. I thought it was likely whatever is happening with you guys."

The *hmmm* sound he made didn't reassure me that he agreed.

"Give me your finger."

I obliged, and he poked me, which I didn't know he was about to do. "Sorry."

He squeezed the blood into a vial and stuck it into the same machine that had my DNA. "This will be faster," he explained.

The machine beeped almost immediately, and he stared down at the screen. "Damn. You seemed fine. I should have known it was the adrenaline masking. Major accident like that." He put out his hand, and I took it.

My heart raced, which made me dizzy. "Am I okay?"

"No, you're very anemic, and I think you might be bleeding internally. We're going to fix that."

I pulled at my hair until it hurt. I couldn't seem to stop. "I hate hospitals. Please don't put me in one. I'll stop bleeding. I just will."

Cole's expression changed, he was suddenly hard to read. Or maybe I simply couldn't understand what I was seeing because of the panic racing through me. I'd run away. He couldn't make me. . .

He drew me to him slowly even as I tried to tug away. "Sshh. Now, don't be afraid. Nothing—I mean nothing— will ever happen to you with me around."

"I hate hospitals. They hurt you there."

My mate nodded slowly. "Orphanage problem or somewhere else? See, Finn taught me that word."

I swallowed. "Orphanage. Good job learning the word."

"You're not going to a hospital. I'm just going to take care of you right here. I like to know that you have these fears though. That'll help me understand when you don't tell me you're feeling sick or have pain in the future. Rather than think you don't trust me." He kissed my head. "All will be well."

I didn't remember anything after that for a long while. I was on the couch in the main room the next time I could really think clearly. My head was in Cole's lap, and my feet were on Rylan's. They were both reading. In a chair across the room, Finn sat reading as well.

"Hey, look who opened her eyes." Cole touched my cheek. "Processing yet, or are we going back under?"

I hated being sick. Disliked every second of it. "Did you go under or are you using we to just be a jackass?"

Cole snorted, and Finn laughed. Rylan shook his head. It was the doctor who answered me. "You did warn me how you lash out. You're all fixed now. Once the medicine that knocked you out wears off, you should feel incredibly better. Thirsty?"

"Oh, don't be mad." Rylan winked at me. "He drugs Finn and me whenever we need it to have operations. You wake up feeling like hell."

Nausea presented itself right then, and I closed my eyes. "I don't want to throw up on the couch."

Finn pushed my legs down and then picked me up. "Good idea. Let's get you to the bathroom. Do you know what else would be a great idea? If you could never, ever do that again. Never have internal injuries that you don't mention again."

"I wasn't in pain."

That didn't seem to matter. I'd done something wrong

in nearly bleeding to death, and it didn't seem they were going to see it any other way.

━━

We'd apparently gone to war, and no one had told me. I'd been on the planet for seven days and with the guys for five of them. I guessed. I wasn't one hundred percent sure on the timeline. My injuries and need to recover had left me pretty much bedridden, and I hated it. The grumpier I got, the happier that seemed to make Cole.

"People start to get aggravated with treatment when they start to feel better. Bears are the same way. You weren't really objecting much that first day. I think. . .I think you were sort of in a slow decline, and then it sped up. I'm just glad I got in there when I did." The bear showed in his eyes. "I have to remember that you're different, slightly more fragile."

He stood by the window, looking outside with me at nothing. We might be attacked at any time, and I was standing inside doing *nothing*. "If you tell me how fragile I am one more time, I'm going to punch you. Hard. Then you can tell me how fragile I am."

Cole side-eyed me. "I have this real issue going on where I find you sexy as hell, but I can't do that because you are still in recovery."

I shoved at him but he didn't move. "This isn't going to work."

"Oh, we're back to that. You spent the last two days not talking. Before that, I was fairly certain you'd warmed to the idea."

My head hurt. "Are you trying to be an asshole? What am I going to do here? I can't be pampered and wander around the house like a. . .I don't know what. . .for the rest of my life. I have to have something to do."

"Get dressed. We're going for a walk."

I hit the wall, which was stupid because it made my hand hurt, but I just didn't feel like being reasonable. That was the most irrational thing I could think to do. I sighed. "Cole."

"If you're going to hit walls, it's going to hurt."

I'd seen very little of Rylan or Finn in the last few days. We were at war, and that apparently meant they were busy. Finn stayed behind closed doors, and Rylan disappeared to wherever he had gone. Not that I could tell we were at war. Everything was quiet, exactly as it had been since I'd arrived.

I put on my clothes that Cole acquired for me when I was laid up and followed him out of the house. The air was warm, and now that I wasn't bleeding inside my body, I wasn't bothered by it. How Cole had operated on me remained a mystery, but since all I could seem to manage was to either be a baby or a bitch, I hadn't asked him about it.

"Where are we going?"

He didn't answer, so I continued to follow him. After a minute, I spoke again. "Going to answer me?"

Cole shook his head. "You'll see where we're going when we get there."

"Hey, I'm injured here, doctor. Could you maybe slow down?"

He whirled around. "Are you in pain?"

"No." I caught up to him. "But you can't go from not letting me move to making me run."

"I can, apparently. I'm doing it right now." He took my hand. "You didn't lose your spleen. It's still in there. You're not bleeding, and I think maybe you need to move your body a bit. Come on. I'm going to show you something you can choose to do if you so decide."

We eventually rounded a corner and came across abandoned houses that had clearly seen better days. Peeling wood, windows hung sideways. Doors swung open and closed in the wind.

"We should have more small-clanned bears living on our land. Like Easton did. Like the two bears following us now do. They're just looking. They mean no harm." I hadn't even known they were there. It was like I was constantly going to be a toddler wandering around with no awareness. A memory rolled over me. These places looked strikingly familiar. This was how they had housed us on the colony on Mars. I sighed. I hadn't thought so much about that year in my entire life as I had managed to do this week.

I pointed at the shacks. "Well, no wonder if this is where they could live when they didn't feel like being the bear."

He put his hands in his pockets and walked forward. "It's important to have more shifters living on our land. They're not just our people that we help take care of, they help us defend this territory during war. Three of our bears are with Rylan right now, holding off would be assailants. Not to worry. It's going just fine."

So the war was taking place. Just in that silent bear fighting way. When they really battled, they didn't make a sound. "I wouldn't want to live in these."

"I know. Me neither. Fix them, would you?"

I blinked. "What?"

"Fix the houses. I don't mean decorate them. They can do that themselves. I mean fix them. You fly spaceships. You lived in the woods." I didn't remember telling him that part, but maybe I did, either before my operation or after. I'd apparently been rambling a lot during recovery. "I bet you are good at building, demolishing, and remodeling."

He wasn't wrong. "I wanted to build a house and live in a lot. Alone."

Cole pointed at the area. "Well, you're not living alone. But you can build houses and people will come to them. We run this planet. I know Finn looks like he's not stressed. But. . ."

I shook my head, stopping him. "Finn is plenty stressed."

"You see that, then. I'm not surprised. You are our mate. Okay. This would help him. Manage everything here. I've got to be more available medically to the population during a fight. Rylan will keep us all safe while Finn leads. In the event of an emergency, we'd all battle. You'll be safe."

I waved my hand. "I've never been safe. You all seem preoccupied with assuring me of my safety. Trust me, it'll be a miracle if I make it without being blown up."

"I think you say that just to make me upset."

I winked at him. "Do I?"

Cole laughed. It was a nice sound. We weren't yelling at each other. I wasn't angry. This was better. I walked toward the shacks. "I can do this."

"I know. So you'll do this. Starting in a week, when your physician thinks it's safe. Walking now, yes. Wielding a hammer, no."

Adorable man. "What about sex? When am I cleared for that? Because I don't have your scent yet, right? That is part of what happens with the sex. I wear you." I touched my shirt. "In my pores."

He visibly swallowed. "Well, I guess it would depend on how rough that got. We've been not so mercilessly giving

Rylan a hard time about how injured you suddenly were after being with him."

It had been a little damaging. And I'd loved every second of it.

"Don't do that." I brought his hand to the outside of my shirt but on my breast. His gaze fell straight to it, and the bear appeared before vanishing. "Yes? No? With the bears that live around here watching?"

He sucked in a long breath. "I'd like to, very much, and I think on the safety end of things, in a soft bed, it's probably okay." He cleared his voice, then added, "You on top so you control things? That's how it works, right?"

"It can." I didn't know what made me talk to Cole the way I was. He seemed to like it. There was color in his cheeks and a noticeable bulge in his pants. "I've never done it that way. So if we were to do it that way, you'd be my first."

He stepped closer to me. "I'd like that."

"Me too." I brought his hand to my neck. I'd never done that before. I knew what I was telling him. Take me. Own me. Out in here in the fresh air, not feeling trapped, that was all I wanted. "I trust you."

He dropped his hand, and my most gentle mate practically dragged me back to our house. I was flat on my back on the bed before I knew what hit me. He kissed me so carefully, keeping himself off of me.

Sometime, he'd have to tell me how he operated. I had no scars, no indication I'd been hurt at all. Still, the few minutes we lay there breathing through our kisses, he was so tentative. Was it my injury or his inexperience?

It didn't matter. I wasn't going to break. Not doing this. I pushed at him until he rolled over. His eyes were huge. "Jessica, love." He breathed heavily. Whatever else he wanted to say, he didn't. That was fine. It wasn't the time for talking.

I undressed him slowly, keeping my own clothes on until the last minute. I liked how he looked at me, I liked the way his gaze followed my every move. I like watching his cock harden.

"You're beautiful." I used a phrase he'd given to me once. "I don't think I told you that."

His nostrils flared. "Jessica, I think you might be tormenting me."

"I am." I rolled over and crawled toward him. "But in the best possible way, right?"

I climbed up his body. There would be time to learn each other, time to figure out each other's bodies. To take him in mouth, as I heard people did, and let him put his mouth on me. I was wet, practically dripping.

I took him deep inside of me, and he cried out. It was a beautiful thing, watching Cole find pleasure for the first time, to experience this with me. I moved, up and down, ever so slowly, and knew the second he was lost to me.

Cole was officially out of his own head. That's where I wanted to be. I took his hands in mine to balance better, and I moved on top of him until we were both panting. Minutes turned. I didn't know how much time had passed. Who cared? This was all that mattered. Fuck, war. Fuck, worry. Fuck, anything else. This was the world. The universe. The everything. I wanted to feel like this every fucking day.

I changed my rhythm so he'd rub more on my clit. That was best at this angle and sure enough, the slow burn of pleasure grew with each pass.

He let go of one of my hands to caress my breast. "Yes, right there. Pinch. Whatever you want."

Cole did as I instructed him. I increased my speed, and

his hand dropped down to my heart. He pressed down on the spot where he could feel it beat. Tears came to my eyes. That was so sweet.

I lost it. Right there. I came in a flurry of pleasure and tears. I couldn't differentiate one from the other. I didn't want to. All of it was right in that moment. As though, by taking Cole inside of me, I finally did come home.

Cole held me for hours. Neither of us slept. The need to constantly sleep was gone from all of us. Whether that was because it was finally warmer or because there was war on our borders, it didn't matter.

I finally voiced a question I'd wanted to ask. "What happens if they overwhelm us? There are so few of you here."

"There are few bears who would want to battle like that. Most bears just want to be left to their own lives. The few that would come here and challenge us won't run through us. But we are not a small number. There are three of us here. Hundreds and hundreds of us out there. One of them told Rylan yesterday that you gave them hope. A quarter of them don't find mates. Maybe they're coming from elsewhere."

I shook my head. "Too much right there for me to deal with. Where do we get our food? Do we hunt, fish?"

"Yes. Sometimes in the cities, they sell it."

I grinned at him. "I'm a really good fisherwoman."

With the sun coming down over my head, I sat near their creek and tried to catch our dinner. We had lots of supplies. An impressive amount, actually. But I wanted to do this, and so far, the guys were letting me.

They were all with me, but I was the only one wielding the fishing rod.

"You could just shift and get them, right? Pick up the fish."

Finn cleared his throat. "Sure. But this is much more impressive."

I rolled my eyes at him. "Don't patronize me. I realize this might be one of those weird things about having me and not a bear shifter. But you picked me. So you're stuck with me now."

Rylan nudged me with his leg. "Nothing stuck about it. You were just what we always wanted. Right, guys?"

Cole kissed my cheek. "Right."

Finn caressed my other cheek. "Everything."

Cole started talking. "I've analyzed your DNA. You're a miracle, Jessica. There might be things I could do to extend your life a little further to match our span. Seems somewhere along the lines, someone in your background was a bear shifter. Really, a long, long time ago. You can't shift or anything. But you could live longer."

I scrunched up my face. "Old? Like I'll have to be in pain longer? Or youthful longer? It makes a difference."

"Healthy. Like maybe you could age as we do. You're twenty-five. You could be one hundred twenty-five."

Rylan put his head in my lap. "Think about it. One hundred years with us."

They were awfully calm. "Isn't there war out there?"

Finn nodded. "There is. And I want some of it. Keep the fish for me, won't you? I'll be back in a couple of hours."

Rylan jumped to his feet. "Wait, Finn. Not alone. Not without me."

Cole nodded at both of them. "Good luck."

"Hey." I put out my arms. "Say goodbye."

Finn's face fell. "We'll be back." Still, he pulled me into a hug. "Don't worry. There are just a few bears I want to show my face to. Let them remember who I am and how I got here."

How he got there? "Didn't you inherit the job from your father?"

Finn shook his head. "No. My father lost it. My mother died, and he was just done. I get it now. I'd already be done."

I wagged my finger at him. "Better not be. You know the whole blowing up thing that I'm likely to do."

Cole groaned behind me, and Rylan laughed.

"I took the job back ten years later. I've held it ever since." He pointed at Rylan and Cole. "With a little help from them and some of our friends, I intend to hold it until my son can take it from me."

His son. I swallowed. "What if I can't have children, Finn? We're not technically the same species."

"You can have kids," Cole supplied. "Remember, I checked your DNA and you already have some bear in there. We'd win the genetic battle in this case. Our kids will shift."

I hadn't even been thinking about kids. This was ridiculous. I might even be pregnant right now. Rylan tugged me to him. "We'll be back tonight. They're just posers out there. They'll run for their lives when they see Finn. Bye." He kissed my cheek. "If you wanted to be naked in bed that would work for me."

I laughed, and Cole shoved Rylan's arm. "She's going to be in bed with me. You two want to go start with the asshats on the edge of our boundary, you can go ahead. I get to stay with our mate and cuddle."

"Boo." Rylan winked at me. "See you later."

Rylan and Finn shifted, vanishing into the woods to go battle. I sighed. "I hate that they're going to fight. I hate that they have to. Why am I such a big deal? It seems I'm going to be living a pretty quiet, peaceful life out here. I won't interfere with how anyone else wants to live their lives."

"People don't like change. They swim the same river their whole life, in the same stream, and they think it's the right way to do it because someone told them it was. Then they get a new piece of information that should adjust how they think. . .and rather than just accepting that as hey, something is new, let's rethink this, they push against it. It scares them. Fear makes people dumb."

I put my hand on his arm. "Then I guess shifters aren't so different from regular humans."

"Your brother is going to be okay."

That was such a shift in conversation I almost didn't follow it. "How?"

Cole leaned against a tree. "We do have some shifters that leave. I mean, we don't talk about it. We're not supposed to want to. But some do."

"Really?" I'd never heard that. "That can't be true."

"How would you know? I mean, unless we shift, you don't know. You could be standing next to one in line and have no idea. Our cousin left. We got in touch with him. He's going to buy your brother out of jail and let him know you're fine. Then Cal can go on with his life, and you can live yours here with us."

I threw my arms around him. "Oh, Cole. Thank you. I mean, Cal won't care what I'm doing, but I promised to get him out. Now I'm not a liar."

He picked me up so that my feet swung off the ground. "You're welcome. Now, how about I shift and get us some fish."

"No." I squirmed until he set me down. "I'm a wonderful fisherwoman. I am going to catch us dinner."

He mock-sighed and sat back down on the ground. "All right, have at it. I'll eat next week. By the way, now that I know what you smell like healthy, I'm never going to miss it if you aren't again. Just wanted to be clear on that."

I leaned over to kiss his chin. "I think you're holding on to something that I'm not. I don't blame you for not knowing I was bleeding. Everything about me was new to you."

His bear showed for half a second in his gaze. "Aren't you supposed to be fishing? Not forgiving me for things you shouldn't forgive me for. I was thinking about how much I wanted you and not what might be wrong with you. I'm better than that."

I shook my head. Cole could be obstinate. He only seemed like the easy going one of the group. "You're not even hungry. You ate yesterday. You could go days. I'm the only one who wants to eat. Sorry. You mated a human. You're going to have to watch me eat over and over and over for the rest of your life."

Cole smirked. "It's a good thing I like to watch you eat. It's sexy. The way your mouth moves."

I kicked him lightly. "You aren't going to distract me. I'm catching dinner."

"I'm going to distract you. I can almost guarantee it."

This was *happy*. For the first time in my life, I knew the feeling. I'd thought I'd had it before on occasion, but I hadn't. Not like this. Not like with these three shifters, who for some reason biology had decided I belonged with. I wasn't going to question it. Not anymore.

CHAPTER 8

I SLEPT PRESSED up to Cole, happily dreaming nonsense in my newly found blissful state, when he jerked next to me. My eyes flew open. "What's the matter? Rylan? Finn?"

I had decided to believe them when they said they were okay. But maybe that had been foolish. Maybe. . .

Cole put his hand on my arm. "They're fine. Almost nothing happening with them. No, one of the bears who lives on our land is giving birth. It's not going well. One of them called out to me to come help her. I've got to go." He rubbed his eyes. "I'm not leaving you here alone."

I forgot sometimes how incredible their hearing was. "Go. I'll be fine here. Do you sense or hear any threats?"

"No, but that doesn't mean I'm going to be stupid about this. You're coming with me. Or. . ." His voice trailed off. "Hold on. Rylan, Finn, I need you to come back." He raised his voice slightly. "I'm going to help June give birth. You're coming back to Jessica now, okay?"

He nodded. "They're on their way. Ten minutes. You'll be alone. I hate to even do that. Maybe I should wait." The whole time he spoke, he got dressed. I sat under the sheet we'd pulled over ourselves and watched, really not able to do anything at all. These were the moments I suspected would always be hard. I didn't like to feel ineffectual. Cole winced. "She's really in terrible pain."

I got up on my knees. "Anyone around who is going to cause problems in the next ten minutes? I mean, I know I snuck up on you guys, but you were still very tired from the winter phase. That is over. Scan with your ears and nose. Shift if you have to. But check. Because if I'm not about to be mauled by a human-hating shifter, you need to get over there and take care of this woman and stop obsessing about me."

Cole furrowed his brow. "No one at all."

"Great. Go."

He held out his hand. "Come with me."

"Not if you ever want me to have children. I. . ." I shook my head. "I can't ever see it before I have to do it. Unless, it's different for your women. This is awful for female humans."

Cole nodded. "No, it's awful everywhere. Okay. Ten minutes. They're already on the move back to you." I hated that they were leaving battle to come back and to babysit me as I slept. Still, this wasn't the time nor place for arguing about it. We'd address what I could expect about being on my own later, maybe when we weren't at war with bears that wanted me dead.

I sighed. Drama had a way of following me.

I made my way downstairs to see Cole leave and then shut the door behind him. I locked it. They never did that, but I was going to if I was alone. Just for good measure. When the other two came back, I'd let them in. In the meantime, I wanted to snack. I'd caught two fish earlier, and we'd eaten them, although I hated the taste. In this case, the fish wasn't the same as any other planet I'd lived on, and I doubted it was going to turn out to be a favorite.

I wanted something sweet. But I wasn't sure they had anything. The porridge was a little, but the guys ate more for functioning than enjoyment. They probably had nothing that resembled chocolate or peanut butter.

I'd found a piece of fruit and eaten it by the time it occurred to me that more than ten minutes had passed. Maybe Cole had misjudged how much time it would take for them to return. I walked over to the window. The night was dark. I couldn't see anything, but I was sure Finn and Rylan would be back any second.

"Don't laugh at me guys," I raised my voice the way that Cole had done. "But, ah, Cole, Rylan, and Finn, if you can hear this I'm kind of worried about you. Cole, they're not back."

I had no idea if they'd heard me. Finn and Rylan had heard Cole, but maybe that was just a bear thing. I chewed on my fingernail and moved away from the window. The clock seemed to be taunting me. Tick. Tick. Tick. Every second a reminder that guys who were probably never late ever got more and more away from their arrival time.

My heart rate kicked up. "Okay, let's think about this, Jessica. Cole is busy. He's helping to deliver a baby. He can't come running back. Besides, he has communicated with that amazing hearing of his with Finn and Rylan. He knows why they're late, and he's unconcerned. They stopped to help a person whose house has flooded." Not that it had been raining. "Or something. They're just delayed. You are going to sit down on the couch and wait without panicking. That is what you are going to do. You aren't this woman. You fly spaceships. You crash landed and survived in the woods. Probably with dumb luck, but there you go. You don't panic."

Maybe if I said it enough, I'd believe it.

I waited. I couldn't even read anything since their books looked like strange symbols, not words. I was going to have to learn to read their language. I'd get to that. Surely, they'd know someone who could help me.

What had I done in the orphanage when I'd been scared? What had I done when I took care of Cal in the woods? What had I done when my uncle made me fly a spaceship years before I was ready to? I didn't know. I couldn't remember a thing. I. . .

The door handle turned. It was locked but that didn't seem to matter. It turned, the sound of breaking metal filling the room. I knew instantly it wasn't one of my mates. They'd never break down their own door. This was. . .someone else.

I had one thought, and it was to run for the safe room. The door flew off its hinges just as I got down the hallway toward Finn's office.

"Jessica," a voice I didn't know called out to me. "Don't run in there. I'm fully aware that I can't get in there. But I'll have to burn the house down with you in it. If you don't do that, you can live through this and so can your mates."

I stopped moving. That was the perfect thing to get me to stop running. Not because I was all that concerned with my own safety. I'd have to be stupid to think I had any chance to live through this unscathed but I couldn't let him harm the guys.

I sighed. I'd been terrified, but as calmness wafted through me, I was suddenly fine. This was an unwinnable, miserable situation, and I knew how to manage this kind of pain. Sudden happiness was something else.

I turned around. "They're already dead if you're here."

"No." He shook his head. He was tall with red hair and a goatee. Not as tall as my mates but not small either. I doubted anyone on this planet would be. "Let me introduce myself. My name is Robert McDermott. I was here earlier in the week to meet with Finn. He wasn't particularly helpful."

This man was the reason I'd been shut in the room to begin with. Cole had said he wasn't to be trusted. He'd clearly been right.

"What have you done with them?"

He sighed. "The problem with your mates, and their fathers before them, is that they care too much about things. One rough pregnancy leads Cole from the house, and your other two mates turn around to come protect you. They've been waylaid. Not dead. Not yet. They don't have to be."

Tears came, but I didn't let them fall. This wasn't the time for grief. "You're going to kill them."

"I'm not. See, I don't want to follow the Derbys. I've always liked the way the Durojos lead. Until recently. I'm not strong enough to hold this planet together, but I am not going to be ignored. Why did Finn have to announce you like you were something everyone should accept? I don't personally have a problem with you. I've known about Mark and his human for a long time. There are at least five families hiding a human. That's all he had to do—hide you. No one had to know."

I really didn't understand. "You like them, so you did this?"

"I want them to lead. I want them to get over this. It's not a true mating. That can only happen with one of their kind."

This man really liked to hear himself speak.

He continued to do so. "They're infatuated. Fine. They'll get over it. And as long as I can prove to them you were returned to your people and not terribly injured, they won't overreact. You can always count on Finn to be reasonable. Or at least we will be able to again. You're going home, Jessica. Your people are taking you back."

"You can't possibly be in contact with them." I started to shake. "Only Finn could do that."

"The Derbys can too. I've convinced them to let you return to them rather than kill you. As soon as you're off this planet, all will be well."

This was happening. McDermott would be faster than me and stronger. I had no way out except death or compliance. "You can't think it'll be that simple."

"Most things are, human. Come with me." He held out his hand. "Make me work for it, and I'll take it out on them. See, they could always beat us physically. They just never saw the knock out drugs coming. Took five darts to take down Rylan. Struggle, and he'll have more than a headache when he comes to."

That sounded right. It would take five to take out Rylan. McDermott dragged me outside. I wasn't done arguing with him. "They'll smell you all over this house. They'll know it was you."

He smiled. "They won't."

As I stood outside watching the one true home I'd ever had blow up, I had to give it to fate. It sure did like to make the things I said sort of true. They were going to think I blew up in an explosion.

Tears rushed down my cheeks.

McDermott had one more thing to say. "I have to tell you that the Derbys will hurt you before they deliver you over. That's just how these things go, my dear. It's a rough planet. Not anywhere that a human like yourself should be living."

I slapped him hard, letting my fingernails dig into his skin. He gasped. "My ancestors were bears you asshole. I have my own claws."

His smile shocked me, but there it was. "Thank goodness you're not boring."

No, I was never that.

I was also royally screwed.

Although, I shouldn't be surprised. This wasn't a fairy tale. I didn't get happy endings.

The Derbys lived hours away, and it was the first time I got the chance to see how shifters got places without shifting and running. They had hover cars. We'd tried this on Earth before I was born, and it hadn't gone well. Maybe the lower population and the fact that everything was so quiet all the time made a difference. People could hear the cars coming. It buzzed loudly, and either McDermott was a lousy driver or the car bounced incessantly too.

I obsessed over my mates. Were they okay? Were they actually dead? Would I know if they were?

I curled up, my head on my knees with my legs pulled up as close into me as I could make them on the seat. Nausea rolled through me. As long as I could stay alive, there had to be hope. The guys would come.

They would.

We'd only known each other a brief period of time and yet. . .I believed.

The Derbys' home was falling apart. I'd been there two days, and they'd done nothing but shout around me. No one spoke to me, but at least I should be grateful I wasn't being beaten or locked in some kind of bear dungeon. There were at least ten clans there all gathered, and their female mates and daughters ran around cleaning as the men drunkenly sloshed through the house, yelling and breaking things—either accidentally or on purpose.

They threw food at me to eat, but other than that, I'd mostly been left alone. If I had to pee, someone took me.

The guy I'd come to think of as the leader, since he was quieter than the others and yet they deferred to him, held my attention. I wondered if part of being a good person in charge required the ability to be quiet and listen a whole lot of the time. Not that I was going to compare this man who was holding me prisoner to Finn.

Time moved slowly. I watched them as they drank. I watched them as they puked. For people who didn't want humans on their planet, they were certainly hypocritical when it came to their behavior. They were hardly keeping themselves pure and neat.

They talked often of my mates. Calling them traitors and saying they had lost sight of what it meant to be a bear. I almost called out to them then; I almost argued.

I was dumb, not stupid. Sometimes, it was just better to keep my damned mouth shut.

But the leader, he watched me. And it really creeped me out. After two days, he finally had something to say.

"I don't like that she can understand us when we speak." The leader got up and walked over to me. "Her people will be able to ask her things about us, and she knows more than she should."

McDermott shrugged. "Too late to do anything about that now. This is almost over."

"Well, she doesn't have to hear anymore."

"How do you propose to. . ."

I never heard what he said. One second, I sat on the floor, watching them converse, the next, the bear I thought was the leader picked me up with one hand. I dangled in his hold, my feet not touching the floor. He hit me in the left ear. Once. Twice. Three times. The world tilted sideways. He didn't just want to hurt me.

He was disconnecting my translator. Breaking it. Three swift hits short-circuited the device. It was a design flaw.

That was the last coherent thing I thought.

The world seemed to scream at me in a tongue I did not speak. My head rang. Everything went black.

▬

"Now, it's time to open your eyes, miss."

I wrenched my lids open. I didn't know where I was, but it wasn't in the Derby's house anymore. I rubbed my eyes? "Where am I?"

"On a spaceship heading back to Earth," an elderly woman spoke to me. "You were concussed, but we fixed that right up with the concussion serum. You're lucky. Almost no one gets away from that savage place."

The gray-haired older lady wasn't just anyone. She was the president of the Union's pilots. One of the first to be paid full time to deliver for them. She was in charge of all of us now, but it was mostly a figurehead position. She didn't fly anymore. What was she doing here with me?

"I. . ." I sat up, and she didn't try to stop me. Dizziness came and went before I could speak again. "What's going on? You're Lara Washington. What are you doing here? I need to go back. My mates. They'll think I'm dead. I have to go back."

She sighed, covering her mouth with her hand for a second. "I'm here because we didn't want a galactic incident over this. I mean, really, dear, can't you have at least the good sense to die if you crash in a place like that?"

I startled. What had she just said? "I. . ."

She waved her hand. "We needed our gold back. The Derbys had you. We aren't to be there. It was easier to take you. As for your mates. . ." She sneered on the last word. "Ten men and women have been rescued from there. It's always mates or mate this and that. No, it's all insanity. Something they do to you. Don't worry. We have the cure."

I jumped off the table. "I don't want to be cured. I love them. Just take me back. You'll never have to worry about me again."

She shook her head. "No. I'm afraid that isn't going to happen."

Two men came through the door. One of them wielding a syringe like a weapon. I didn't rush to get away from them. Where would I go? I sighed. Numbness struck me before I was ever poked with the needle that I was sure would put me back to sleep. Lara had wanted me awake long enough to deliver the bad news that I was truly fucked. Awful kind of her.

I was never going to see my mates again. Even on the planet, I had managed to maintain some hope. But that was gone now. They couldn't find me out here. Some bears might travel through space, but my guys didn't. And who knew where I'd ultimately end up?

They were going to put me somewhere I'd never be able to tell anyone about Planet Bear. About matings. About whatever might make people interested in a place we weren't to go.

I turned to the gentleman holding the syringe. "Do you suppose that it was better I knew what love felt like once or would it have been better never to know it?"

He didn't give me an answer. That wasn't surprising. The needle stung.

———

Of all the places I'd expected to spend time during my life, an asylum hadn't been one of them. Nope, not at all. I supposed I shouldn't have been surprised, but six months since I'd been dumped here, informed I was crazy for thinking that I was mated and that they were going to fix me, I wasn't any less shocked.

Maybe I was nuts. Maybe I was mentally deficient because I couldn't get my head around the sheer lunacy of this.

I laughed, and the orderly shook his head. Yep, I was having full-fledged conversations with myself. They'd made me crazy since they locked me up. Oh sure, I wasn't looking at bars like in a prison cells, but it turned out there were lots of ways to be confined against one's will.

This was one of them.

Across the hall was a woman they'd pulled off Wolf Planet. She rambled a lot and rocked. Screamed for her mate. Just one. . .

They were drugging her more than me because I made less noise. That seemed to be the key. Don't give the doctors, nurses, or orderlies a headache, and you don't have to live your life in chemically induced misery.

What was really weird was how I could still see my bears in my mind. As though I could touch them if I just tried hard enough. I'd given it a go a few times now, and it hadn't helped. No, on this hellish man-made moon circling Earth, I couldn't reach them. No matter how hard I tried.

My hearing was going. Day by day it got worse. Whatever the Derby asshat had done, I was having trouble hearing even the most basic things. The doctors said I was crazy. They wouldn't fix me. Soon, I'd not have to hear a thing anyone said to me.

I threw down the pudding I'd been trying to eat. They were probably gone. I hoped that wasn't true. That thought was the only thing left that could make me cry. They had to think I was dead.

That meant they'd be gone now. I wiped at my eyes. Mates didn't outlive each other very long. I curled up in a ball. I was done with today's hell. I wouldn't tell my captors that my mating didn't happen. It did.

I'd never deny it. I'd die first.

Six months earlier
Finn

I crawled to my feet, stumbling twice. Rylan was out cold, but he wasn't dead. I listened to the woods. Nothing. No sound of battle. No sound of Cole calling for us. What in the hell had happened?

"Brother." I shook him slightly, and he moaned. It

would have taken a lot of whatever we'd been struck with to bring us both down.

I couldn't even remember what happened. It didn't matter. Someone had taken us down, and that meant this whole area was at risk. Why? This wasn't how we warred.

"Rylan." I shook him again. "Up. Now. Need you."

His eyes opened slowly. He sat up and scrunched up his face. "What in the fuck happened?"

"Not sure. I. . ."

A roar sounded in the night. It was half bear, half man and all of it pain. I knew the sound instantly. That was Cole. In horrific grief. I was running before I even realized. I shifted mid-stride. I'd be faster as a bear, and my bear wouldn't let me down. He'd get to Cole.

As a bear, I didn't have to think, so I didn't. He and I both knew what could make Cole sound like that. There were only three people on the planet that would warrant that response, and I knew Rylan and I were fine.

I arrived at the house, shifting into my human form. Cole was on his knees, and our home was. . .gone, burning, a pile of rubble on fire. Why hadn't I smelled it?

"The drugs." Rylan answered. It must have been his first question too.

Cole pointed at the burning mess, his hand shaking. I'd make this fine. "It's okay. We can build a new one."

I never gave a shit about stuff. It was all just. . .I whirled around. Where was Jessica? We needed to block her from the flames. She'd feel the heat more than we would.

On Cole's face, I saw reflected the realization that my brain refused to acknowledge. "She's in there."

Cole nodded. "I left her here .You were supposed to be coming back. Ten minutes. I. . .I got struck with something. It knocked me out. I. . ."

"Us too." Rylan's voice broke. "We have to get her out. She can't make it in there much longer."

Rylan rushed to the flames. I grabbed him. He wasn't thinking. None of us were. "She's not alive."

I said the words, and then I joined Cole on the ground. Our little human had just burned to death. Had it been an explosion? I looked up. How would I know, and what did it matter? My girl was gone. We just had her. How could. . .

I roared to bring down the heavens. The space. Sky. I didn't care. Rylan wanted to run into the flames, and fuck it, so did I. If she was in there, I'd be there too.

"Commander." A voice from the woods called out to me. Bronson? What in the hell did he want?

I couldn't answer him. Maybe he'd understand, maybe he wouldn't.

"She was taken. I watched. I should have stopped him. But. . .he's so violent. I thought if I did save her, then it would be worse. He took her."

Bronson rambled a lot. His brain had been addled in a war. He'd never been quite the same since. Cole and Rylan watched him with rapt attention while I managed to pull myself up one more time.

"Who took her?"

I'D ALWAYS BELIEVED the thing about being a bear was that when we battled, it would be a fair fight. At the end of the day, we struck at one another and the stronger bear walked away. Even when my mother had died during a war, it had been shifted as a bear, fighting to protect her home. She had lost that day. Maybe most of that responsibility fell on my fathers' shoulders. But it had been a fair fight that hadn't gone our way.

What McDermott did, taking our mate—hitting us with poison darts, knocking us out, and faking her death after burning our home—it wasn't what bears did. We all had the souls of a bear pressed inside of us. How did his bear live with it?

In any case, my own bear was perfectly comfortable with what we were doing. Revenge made us both happy.

If I'd been shifted, I might have even started to tear him apart while he still lived. Piece by piece. I might have seen how long I could keep him alive while I did that. It might have made the whole act sweeter.

As it was, he was strapped to a medical table able to

hear the Derbys dying in the other room. Finn wanted him dead, and he wanted to do it himself. It was hard to restrain my bear from doing what he would do naturally—kill any that hurt his mate. But we were waiting.

In the meantime, he was terrified. The scent wafted through the room, and that was something. Not enough. But something.

Rylan walked in. He stared at the whimpering McDermott and looked back at me. "Surprised he's still alive."

"Our clan leader asked me to let him kill him. I am doing as I was asked." I clenched my jaw. I didn't know if I was ever going to stop feeling this angry. How could I ever let it go? The emotion overpowered everything.

Someone shouted from the other room, and Rylan put his hand on my back. "Go. I've killed my share. You can go take yours. I'll watch our betrayer. At least with the Derbys, they never came to the house, they never pretended to be anything other than what they were."

"I was trying to save this planet," he called out from the bed. Rylan lifted his eyebrows.

I ignored McDermott. "You're controlling the bear."

"Looks like it."

That was great news. We could celebrate another time.

Okay, my brother Finn could manage this piece of shit on the table. I had enemies to end. Yes, my bear liked that. I strode into the room ready to shift. There were four bears other than my brother, and two of them cowered in the corner. That wasn't enough of a challenge. Finn turned to look at me. As a grizzly, he always looked like he was in impressive control. He'd so terrified those two bears that they weren't even trying to fight?

He stepped back. Yes, he understood. I needed this. Jessica was my mate. She had fallen from the sky, and she was mine. She belonged to our clan. She and no one else would have my cubs should such a thing happen. I would not live in a universe without her.

And all of these fuckers could die.

I could heal. But I could also kill.

Tonight was about the second.

━━━

Rylan

I listened to the sounds of death from the other room. Cole would end the only two bears worth fighting, and he'd do it fast. Finn had started to taunt them. That meant it was time to change gears. I kept them all safe, and sometimes that was against their worst selves. Finn could be cruel, mean, to those he deemed unworthy of his time. These lesser beings had taken our mate.

He needed to get down to it so we could get information from McDermott. All he had said was he would end the man. He hadn't said anything about who was going to get the information.

I smiled at McDermott, and he paled. Yes, that was right. He saw death in my eyes.

I put my hand on his stomach. "How long do you think you could live if I cut you here?" I wasn't shifted. In that state, my claws were always out. That didn't mean I couldn't hurt him. I grabbed a knife. It looked like one someone might use in the kitchen. Why did the Derbys have this stuff in their medical room? I shrugged. They didn't have anything anymore. They were all very, very dead.

Finn walked into the room, still a bear. He stood by the doorway, tilting his head. Okay, if he didn't want to shift and do this just yet, I would.

"Where is my mate?"

McDermott's mouth shook which made it hard for him to speak. "Your mating can't be real. She's human. You're simply infatuated with her because of her blonde hair and blue eyes."

Oh, I was done with this. I put the knife through his hand. He shouted, roaring with pain, the bear in his eyes. He wasn't going anywhere. Not strapped the way Cole had him. "Try again."

We would get to her. As fast as we could. This man was going to give up his information. And I was going to make it hurt.

A lot.

Jessica
One year in the asylum

An alarm blared, waking me slightly. It had to be extremely loud for me to hear it, but what did it matter, really? They'd drugged me for crying too much. That was okay. They kept me like this, and it was better. All the fight was out of me. I rolled over. Someone would turn off that alarm soon. Maybe it was a mind game set to screw with some of the rebels they had here. Funny thing was that I hadn't even known there were rebels. Who rebelled? Who cared that much about the dang Union?

I shut my eyes. A minute later, I was shaken awake.

Groaning, I forced myself to rise to the surface of consciousness.

I had to be seeing things. It looked like Rylan, Cole, and Finn stood right over me. Behind them there was chaos. Inmates running everywhere. What a weird dream. I closed my eyes.

I was picked up. That was fine. I didn't have to think about where I was going or if I could walk there. The meds kept me off balance. That was because I'd tried to run away. Couldn't do that if you couldn't walk. . .

They had an injection for everything.

My head throbbed, and some time passed. Where was the orderly with my daily feel-nothing pill? I'd take it now. I wouldn't even object. I could just. . .

I opened my eyes. Cole stood over me. He wiped my head with a cool cloth.

"Dream?" I'd started to shout what I said, I thought. I couldn't hear myself unless I did.

He scrunched up his face, and although he said something, it was too low for me to hear it. It didn't sound like words, just mumbligook. Like any language that wasn't my own now sounded.

"Look, dream, I can't hear you. They broke me. My hearing is all but gone, I can't speak bear, and my translator is gone too. I'm broken." I waved at his hand when he tried to wipe at me again. "If you can still understand me, go away. I don't like to see them. It's nothing but pain."

The dream of Cole didn't listen and instead, continued to talk too low for me to hear. He was insistent on wiping my face with the cloth. I bet if I could hear him, it would be soothing. Finn appeared, standing next to him. They opened and closed their mouths, clearly discussing something, and Cole rose to walk over to the medicine cabinet.

Oh no. This dream had taken a decidedly nightmarish turn. I liked my drugs just as they were. The cocktail I was on didn't need to be altered, and I didn't need any more injections. I threw myself off the medical table. Or I would have, if Finn hadn't caught me.

He pressed his lips to my temple, and he made noises I couldn't understand. This was so ridiculous. I was on a spaceship in this scenario, and my guys never would be. Rylan came through the door. He shouted unintelligible sounds, but at least I could hear how he made them.

Finn shouted something back, and then he rocked me in his arms. After I stopped trying to get away, it was sort of soothing.

Rylan came to the side of us and put his hand on my cheek. Were there tears in his eyes? There shouldn't be. They didn't cry in my dreams. They were free. Running as bears. No more nonsense.

No more war.

Then Cole was back, still holding that injection. I closed my eyes. I was through fighting the inevitable. Okay, he was going to hurt me. There was going to be a pounding right in my arm. But he was gentle. It pinched, and then it was over. A coolness passed through my arm. Whatever he put in me didn't hurt like the way the abusive drugs did.

I wasn't out cold. It didn't knock me on my rear. More like. . .I crawled against Finn. Letting him hold me closer. Cole touched my ear, and it didn't hurt. That was weird. Anytime anyone came anywhere near it, I hollered in pain. He shined a light in it, and I could hear his voice as he spoke to Finn and Rylan. I couldn't understand him, but that close to my ear, I could hear him.

This was starting to feel very real.

"Dreams shouldn't be this real. That makes them harder to leave."

Rylan stroked the top of my head. To make matters even stranger, my brother came through the door.

"What's the prognosis?" I could understand him just fine.

I sat up a little, and Cole put his hand on me to stop me. He answered Cal, but I couldn't understand him.

"Okay, then. See you in a bit, Jess. Love you."

Love me? He didn't love me. No one loved me.

All three of my mates spoke. Maybe I'd said that last part aloud.

"Can you understand me and hear me?" Cole brushed my hair off my forehead. I sweated badly. It was hot in here. Or maybe it was just the furnace that was Finn holding me.

"I can." I squirmed, and Finn let me up just a little. He still had his arm around me. "How is this happening?"

Rylan scooted over from where he'd been leaning by the wall. "Fuck, yes."

I rubbed at my eyes. "I don't understand."

Cole grinned at me for a second before his head fell down like his neck couldn't support the weight. He took a deep breath and lifted it. "Your translator was damaged. No one fixed it. A side effect of a damaged translator left in the ear is that it makes the person hard of hearing. Worse and worse. I simply had to change it out. Not a big deal. I'm sorry they didn't do it for you. They were all of them butchers and. . ." He didn't finish whatever he was going to say. He rubbed his eyes.

They'd all lost weight since I last saw them, and I had a million questions.

"How is this possible?"

Rylan sat down on the edge of the table. "After we found out you weren't dead, we tracked down McDermott. You'd been gone three days. He's not breathing air anymore. Neither are any of the Derbys."

I swallowed that information and found it didn't bother me at all. "Okay." I pointed to my ear. "Their leader is the one who hurt me with the translator."

Finn snarled. "I wish I could kill him again."

"We got ahold of our cousin, and he came and got us. We were on our way to Earth, working out a plan on how to get to you, not even knowing where you were, when we got a message from your brother. Well, he found us. Turned out he knew our cousin. Nefarious personalities run in crowds." Rylan smiled at the memory. "He knew where you were. Was planning on getting you and wanted to know if we wanted in. He knew who we were, thanks to our cousin."

This all made sense. I hadn't hallucinated seeing Cal. "I. . .I never thought." I choked on a sob and then tugged it back in. They all made varying degrees of growls and whimpers. "I thought that was that. I'd never see you again."

Finn sucked in a long breath. "We failed you." He hit the ground on his knees, his head lowered. "We can't make it right. There isn't fixing this. There is only what can come next. Do you want a future with us? We cannot live in the world if you aren't okay, but if we know you are okay, we will leave you alone. If that is what you wish."

Is that what I wished? "I have wanted nothing but you for. . ." I didn't know how long it had been. "How long since we saw each other?"

Cole sighed. "A year and one day. We were hoping to

get you yesterday, but things aren't moving as fast as we keep trying to make them. We're a bit of a slow moving cog."

"Why?" My ears were working, and suddenly the sound of the ship we flew on overwhelmed my senses. It had been such a long time since I'd been in space, and I used to spend almost every waking moment there. My trip to the asylum didn't matter. I'd been knocked out for most of it. This was a large ship. This was. . .

"Are we on a freighter? Why is this ship so big?"

Rylan put out his hand. "Before we left, Finn gave the people a choice. They could stay where they were and live a completely isolationist life, potentially never finding their mates or they could come with us. It would be a long time until we found a new home, but they could come."

Finn got to his feet, hugging me to him. I could hear his heartbeat. Both of those facts—his heartbeat being near me and that I could hear it—were large miracles.

"I thought maybe Mark would show up with his mate and brothers. We had a larger group than we initially thought. Hence the large ship. There are actually four ships."

Goosebumps broke out on my arms, and I rubbed them away. "That's huge. You guys don't like to leave home, mostly. Where are we going?"

"We've been focused on getting to you. But your brother helped some of the others find a planet he knew about. Terraformed fifty years ago. Apparently, there are all kinds of people there. Shifters, and others who prefer to simply be left alone. We're going to go there now."

My planet on the edge of the universe. Yes, sure, Cal knew about it. I'd talked about it a million times. That's where I was supposed to be going when I got him out of jail.

I nodded. "You had to change your entire planet to be with me. I don't know if I can ever live up to expectations."

Rylan kissed my hand. "No expectations. Just you. Just us. We're not even going to try to lead once we're there. We're just going to be. Just family."

Tears streamed from my eyes. "And can we have a house where the chairs are too big? And the bed is too big? And the fridge has some items I can't identify in it?"

"Maybe we can make some of that furniture just right." Rylan put his nose on my neck, like he breathed me in. Cole kissed my cheek while Finn pressed our foreheads together. That was just what I needed. So we stayed like that. For a very long time.

━━━

One year later

I watched in amusement as the third bear shifter of the morning arrived to ask my mates for advice. Their idea about not leading had been ridiculous. Everyone wanted to know what they thought all the time about all sorts of matters.

This one had to do with the distribution of crops. I wasn't sure that Cole exactly knew that, but he was answering just the same.

I put my hand on my stomach to feel the baby move. We only took up such a small portion of the planet, not wanting to cause issues with our neighbors. Rylan estimated it was maybe an eighth of the place. But with all the babies that were going to be born in the next year, that was bound to increase a bit.

Finn walked over and sat down next to me on our big bench. It had sort of become a joke. We made everything just slightly too big for me. Rylan arrived a second later. They'd seen me watch the suns set on this planet every day since we got here like it was my job.

"There's been something I've wanted to ask you guys since day one."

Cole ran over and sat on the edge of the bench. "Go. I'm here. Ask."

Rylan rolled his eyes. "I bet we could have answered it without you."

"Yes, I'm sure, but not as well as I'm going to answer it."

Finn nudged me. "Ask. They'll do it all night."

"Why did the wolves shoot at me that day? Why did they do that when I wasn't off the set path?"

Finn shrugged. "Who knows with wolves? They're such miserable creatures. Not like the bear. The loyal, understandable, trustworthy bear."

I held back my laugh. He might sound like he was kidding, but he wasn't. If I laughed, he'd try to prove his point, and then we'd be talking about bears for the rest of the night.

Cole nodded. "Never could trust a wolf."

Rylan drummed his hand on the bench. "Besides, if they hadn't done that, you'd never have fallen from the sky and into my lap."

Every time he talked about my crash landing, he added something to it to make the whole thing sound much more romantic than it was.

"That poor ship *Goldie*. She got me down safely."

Finn played with a stand of my golden hair. "We can

tell the kids stories about her someday. That's what life is, right? A retelling of beautiful stories over and over? I can't think of any I like more than the time Jessica arrived on Planet Bear."

I wasn't getting away without hearing about bears tonight. I leaned back on my bench and watched the orange redness of the sky. Finn started talking. Cole would be next. Rylan would finish. I was Jessica, and these were my three bears.

AFTERWORD

―

Thank you so much for reading Planet Bear (Shifter's World #1). If you have a second, I'd very much appreciate a review. Reviews help authors get the word out about their books. Please be on the lookout for Planet Cat, coming soon. Also, I'd love to stay in touch with you! If you are on Facebook, please consider joining me in my reader's group, Rebecca's Randomness, where we talk about books every day:

https://www.facebook.com/groups/458490741256283/

I'll probably talk about Planet Cat in there first....

Do you like science fiction romance? I have a science fiction romance series that you might enjoy. Find the first book, Kidnapped By Her Husbands, here:

https://amzn.to/2MUnTu3

Like shifters? I have a completed Wolf Shifter series called the Westervelt Wolves. You can find it here:

https://amzn.to/2NlOpMl

Please turn the page to find the complete list of all of my books...

ABOUT THE AUTHOR

As a teenager, I would hide in my room to read my favorite romance novels when I was supposed to be doing my homework. I hope, these days, that my parents think it was worth it.

I am the mother of three adorable boys and I am fortunate to be married to my best friend. I live in Austin Texas where I am determined to eat all the barbecue in town.

I am in love with science fiction, fantasy, and the paranormal and try to use all of these elements in my writing. I've been told I'm a little bloodthirsty so I hope that when you read my work you'll enjoy the action packed ride that always ends in romance. I love to write series because I love to see characters develop over time and it always makes me happy to see my favorite characters make guest appearances in other books.

In my world anything is possible, anything can happen, and you should suspect that it will.

I'd love to hear from you! Please visit my website at www.rebeccaroyce.com to sign up for my newsletter and learn about my books!

Here's where you can find me online:

www.rebeccaroyce.com

Rebecca's Randomness Reading Group
https://www.facebook.com/groups/458490741256283/

https://www.facebook.com/authorrebeccaroyce/

www.twitter.com/rebeccaroyce

Instagram: rebeccaroyce79
Cheers!!
Rebecca

Turn the page for a complete list of my books...

Eternal

Always

Evermore

Endless

Wards and Wands

Hexed and Vexed

Curse Reversed

Meow, Baby (novella, Coming Soon in Petting Them antho written with Ripley Proserpina)

Tragic Magic (Coming Soon)

Safe Haven

Everywhere and Nowhere

Dimension X (coming soon)

More coming soon....

Soul Bound

Prisoner of the Dragons

More coming soon....

Shadow Promised

Strange Days

Weird Nights

Bizarre Years

More coming soon...

The Warrior (completed series)

Initiation

Driven

Subversive

Redemption

Justice

Warrior World (spin off of The Warrior, completed series)

Deacon

Micah

Jason

The Westervelt Wolves (completed series)

Her Wolf

Summer's Wolf

Wolf Reborn

Wolf's Valentine

Wolf's Magic

Alpha Wolf

Angel's Wolf

Darkest Wolf

Lone Wolf

Fallen Alpha

Alpha Rising

Alpha's Strength

Alpha's Sacrifice

Alpha's Truth

Alpha Enticing

Hidden Alpha (coming soon)

The Capes (completed series)

Seductive Powers

Adrenaline Rush

Last Ascension

The Conditioned

Eye Contact

Embraced

Unlawful (coming soon...)

The Outsiders

Love Beyond Time

Love Beyond Sanity

Love Beyond Loyalty

Love Beyond Sight

Love Beyond Expectations

Love Beyond Oceans

Love Beyond Flames

Love Beyond Lies (coming soon)

Cascade (completed series)

Haunted Redemption

Phoenix Everlasting

Fragility Unearthed

Persuasion Enraptured

Reverse Harem Story (completed series)

Unconventional

Unexpected

Undeniable

Kiss Her Goodbye

Sacrificial Lamb (coming soon)

Martyrs

Saints

Stand Alone Titles

Planet Bear

Under The Lights

No Quitting Allowed

Mr. Wrong

Bite Marks

Bitten Surrender

The Vampire and The Virgin

Demon Within

Crimson Lust

Call Me Crazy (coming soon)

Writing with Ripley Proserpina

The Storm
Lightning Strikes (coming soon)
Thunder Rolling

www.ingramcontent.com/pod-product-compliance
Lightning Source LLC
Chambersburg PA
CBHW011435170626
46808CB00010B/3182